LOOKING

FOR

JACK

KEROUAC

Also by Barbara Shoup

Young Adult Books

Wish You Were Here
Vermeer's Daughter
Stranded in Harmony
Everything You Want

Adult Books

Night Watch
Faithful Women
An American Tune

Looking for Jack Kerouac

A novel

Barbara Shoup

LACEWING BOOKS
INDIANAPOLIS

Lacewing Books
an imprint of Engine Books
PO Box 44167
Indianapolis, IN 46244
lacewingbooks.org

The Brain Flower typeface, created by Denise Bentulan, is licensed for commercial use with her permission.

Also available in eBook formats from Lacewing Books.

Printed in the United States of America

10   9   8   7   6   5   4   3   2   1

ISBN: 978-1-938126-47-5

Library of Congress Control Number: 2014944273

For Sam and David
Jackie's Boys

For Sherry —
Happy Reading!

ONE

It wasn't Duke Walczak's fault that I took off for Florida, like Kathy thought. The truth is, we started getting sideways with each other on our class trip to New York and Washington D.C. nearly a year earlier—which, looking back, is ironic since she was the one dead set on going.

Not that I wouldn't have loved to go...*anywhere*, especially New York, if I could have gone on my own and just wandered, searching for the places I'd read about in books. But I didn't like hanging out with big groups of kids at home, so why would I want to hang out with them in New York? And, believe me, two days of lockstep sightseeing once we got there didn't change my mind about that. Not to mention our tour guide talking us senseless, determined to tell us every single thing she knew.

The Empire State Building, the U.N., Wall Street, the Statue of Liberty.

Kathy was thrilled. She "adored" the touristy nightclub with its sad, made-up girls in sequins and feathers; she was enthralled by Chinatown and the tour of NBC Studios; she went nuts over the Rockettes. Over and over again: Kathy being rapturous about whatever there was to be rapturous about, then the perfectly posed snapshot, the mind-numbing search for the perfect postcard for her scrapbook and the perfect souvenir.

On our last day in the city, we had a few free hours in the morning, and what Kathy wanted to do was have breakfast at Tiffany's, like in the movie. So we bought a bag of donuts and walked over to Fifth Avenue so she could eat one, gazing at the diamonds in the window, standing exactly where Audrey Hepburn had stood.

When we got there, she handed me her camera. She posed. I framed her in the lens, clicked: Kathy in her pleated skirt and matching sweater, the circle pin with the pearl on it that I'd gotten her for her birthday at the collar, her brown hair in a perfect flip. She's holding up a donut in one hand, her other hand is gesturing toward the window of sparkling jewelry behind her. She's smiling.

In the picture she took of me next, I'm not. I was tired of eating crappy food, tired of sleeping in a roll-away bed in our crappy hotel, tired of being talked to death by tour guides, tired of my moronic classmates and of Kathy herself—and dreading three more days of it in Washington D.C. *The Fugitive* was on TV that night, and I'd have been perfectly happy to stay in and watch it. But Kathy wanted to go to Greenwich Village with some friends—a place I'd read about and would have been high on my list if I could have gone alone. But I didn't want to go with Kathy because I figured there was no way she was ready for it.

Sure enough, she was grossed out from the second we stepped off the subway. First by the smell of urine in the station, then the trash skittering along the street, the bums passed out in shadowy doorways. There were galleries with paintings of naked women in the windows.

The others agreed: We should leave, go back to our hotel, stay safe. But I felt a weird electric buzz from the moment I stepped off the subway and came up into the street. The white, shining arch at the foot of Washington Square, coffeehouses swirling with smoke, strains of folk music pouring into the night. People talking, arguing as they hurried past—beatniks, some of them! Guys with pointy beards, pale girls with long, straight hair—wearing jeans and black sweaters, battered green Army jackets buttoned up against the chilly October evening. Plus, I'd read *The Catcher in the Rye* not all that long before and I was getting a kick out of thinking about Holden Caulfield taking the cab down here to Ernie's Jazz Club after dancing with the tacky girls in the Lavender Room.

"I don't want to go back yet," I said to Kathy. "But go ahead, if you want to."

"Without *you?*"

"Sure. Don't worry, I'll be back by curfew."

She folded her arms across her chest and glared at me.

"What?" I said.

"You're going to leave me *alone?*"

"I'm not leaving you alone," I said. "For Pete's sake, what's the big deal? If you want to go back to the hotel, just get on the subway and go with everyone else."

"Paul," she said.

"I'm staying, okay? You can stay with me if you want, or you can go."

She didn't answer.

Then I did something I'd never done before. I turned and walked away from her.

If she'd come after me, I probably would have done the decent thing and taken her back to the hotel. But she didn't come after me and, the truth was, once I reached the end of block and turned the corner without having felt the touch of her hand on my shoulder or heard her voice call out to me, I didn't think about her the rest of the evening.

I walked the streets of the Village, my shoulders hunched, feeling like the Indiana rube I was. I had on khakis and the maroon cardigan sweater with gray stripes up the front that my mom bought me for the trip. A white tab-collar shirt. My navy blue London Fog jacket. I had the regulation team crew cut. Nobody seemed to notice me, though, and after a while I straightened up and walked more like I belonged there. I walked down MacDougal Street, over on Bleecker, back up toward Washington Square, where bums shared benches with kids my own age who were smoking, laughing, making out.

I could live here, I thought—which shocked the shit out of me. Emboldened, I walked into a tavern, sat down on a barstool.

"Pabst on draft," I said. What my dad always ordered.

The drinking age was eighteen in New York, and I guess I looked close enough because the bartender drew the beer and set a foaming mug before me.

It was good. Ice cold, prickly in my throat.

I liked breaking the rule. I liked thinking there were other rules I could break, too. I was alone in New York City. I knew nobody. Nobody knew me. There was nothing to stop me from doing anything I wanted to do. But I wasn't crazy. I wasn't going to risk doing something really stupid. So I had one more beer, and with a nice little buzz on I stepped out into the city again, satisfied to wander.

I found a battered copy of *On the Road* in a secondhand bookshop that night. There was a dark-haired guy on the cover, his hands in the pockets of his khaki pants, staring out at whoever might pick up the book, with this look on his face like, I dare you to buy it. There were images surrounding him, like a dream—people drinking, dancing, kissing, fighting. A car, a cactus, the shadow of a guy playing a sax.

The bottom of the cover said: "This is the bible of the 'beat generation.'"

I bought the book, stuck it my jacket pocket, and headed toward the subway station. I started reading it on the train, stayed up half the night in the hotel lobby reading. I read during breakfast and on the train to Washington, D.C., only half aware that Kathy was punishing me for the night before by sitting with her girlfriends. When I finished it, I went back to the beginning and read it straight through again.

It was so wild and beautiful. Weirdly familiar, too. Like Sal in the book, I *saw* things. I was moved by them. I remembered, for example, standing on the front porch of our house one summer night when some petroleum tanks at Standard Oil caught fire. I was maybe eight. The fire was miles away, in Whiting, but we could see smoke billowing and orange flames shooting into the sky. Neighbors were slack-jawed on their porches. Some crying. My own parents murmuring anxiously about how many people might be hurt or lose their jobs or even die.

I was dazzled by the fire, my heart beating so hard I thought it would burst right out of my chest. Looking, *looking*—as if I were somehow responsible for capturing the spectacle of it forever.

I wanted like Sal wanted, too—I didn't even know what I wanted. I just *wanted*. Maybe everything. It was like an ache sometimes, that wanting. I never mentioned it. There wasn't a single person in my life who'd have understood, even if I had been able to explain it—and I doubted I could. But lost in the pages of *On the Road*, I felt like…myself. Like the book knew who I was, knew what I wanted, and was speaking back to me somehow.

I took it with me wherever I went. I read while I was supposed to be appreciative of our American government in action, the Smithsonian, the Lincoln Memorial. I finished it, then read it again. And again. All the way back to Indiana, glancing up sometimes to see whole chunks of Pennsylvania and Ohio glide by outside the window, roads running along the track, winding out toward the horizon, and thinking how cool it would be to set out to explore America the way Sal Paradise did in that book. Put out my thumb out and see where life might take me.

During this time, Kathy went from ignoring me to haranguing

me to crying. She sent her girlfriends as envoys to walk past and give me the evil eye. She consulted with my friends, a few of whom came over and sat beside me for a while and asked stupid questions, like, "Hey, man, what are you reading?"

As opposed to what they were actually thinking: "Hey, man, how come you suddenly stopped being so pussy-whipped?"

Kathy and I had one conversation about *On the Road*. We were standing at my locker the first morning back at school, and she saw me take it from the pocket of my letter jacket and tuck it between my physics and English books.

She said, "You know, Paul, that book is banned."

I said, "So what? It's a great book. Maybe you ought to read it and decide for yourself."

Her eyes narrowed. "I don't need to read it," she said. "It's on that list of books Father McNally said we're not supposed to read, and that's good enough for me."

She barely spoke to me the rest of the day.

Mom had caught a bad cold while we were gone, and now she was in bed with an ear infection that made her so dizzy she couldn't walk. So I used the fact that I was helping out at home as an excuse not to see Kathy in the evenings—not that she seemed to want to see me all that much. She went to a slumber party Friday night. We went to a movie Saturday night and got into a stupid argument about it at the Big Wheel afterward.

"Just take me home," she said, when we got in the car to leave.

So I did.

I was *this* close to breaking up with her. I knew what Kathy wanted, ultimately: marriage, kids, a nice house—and the sooner the better. But I'd felt the whole world crack open in New York. I felt changed. I wanted to keep changing and see who I might turn out to be, which was not going to happen as long as I was Kathy's boyfriend. I think I *would* have broken up with her if it had turned out that my mom was okay. But Sunday, she woke up with a terrible headache, so bad she didn't go to mass. Any kind of light hurt her eyes, so she stayed in bed all day, the room as dark as we could make it. First thing Monday, Dad called the doctor, who changed the medicine she'd been on.

It didn't help much. She was still dizzy. The headache didn't go away. Over the next few days she'd smile when Bobby and I came into the bedroom after school to sit with her or to see if there was anything she needed, but I could tell it hurt to move her face. She let out a quiet little sound sometimes, like a baby whimpering in its sleep. Dad called the doctor again, when her headache got so bad she was crying.

"Bring her to the emergency room," the doctor said; he'd take a look at her. Mom tried to reassure Bobby and me that she'd be all right, but she looked scared—and we had to help her to the car, because by then she could barely walk. Dad called an hour later to say they'd given her something for the pain and she was resting comfortably, but they'd decided to observe her overnight and do some testing in the morning. He'd stay there with her.

Kathy was waiting by my locker when I got to school the next morning. Her mom had a friend who was a nurse and who'd called to tell her that my mom had been admitted to the hospital.

"Is she going to be okay, Paul?" she asked.

"They're running tests today," I said. "That's all I know."

She put her arms around me, drew me close. "She'll be okay, she *will*. I'm sorry I've been so awful lately," she whispered. "I love you. I love you so much."

And we moved on into the day as if nothing had happened between us. She came to the hospital with me and Bobby after school, she was there when Dad returned from his conference with the doctors and said, "Your mom has a brain tumor," in a voice I'd never have recognized if he hadn't been standing right there in front of me.

What can I say? Kathy was as stand-up as anyone could have

been in the months my mom was sick. In the spring, after Mom died, she fixed dinner at our house every single night for me and Dad and Bobby. She wasn't a great cook, but she tried—and she cleaned up after us like Mom never did. We'd leave the breakfast dishes in the sink, and she'd do them before starting to make the evening meal.

I should have seen that she was practicing being my wife, that the fantasy wedding she'd been talking about ever since we'd started going steady in the eighth grade had become reality when we graduated and I took the job at the steel mill instead of going right to college like my mom had wanted me to do. I didn't, though. I was on the road, all right—to Kathy's idea of happily ever after. I barreled on a while, her apparently willing bridegroom, and there's no doubt in my mind that if I hadn't met Duke Walczek I'd be on it still.

TWO

Duke and I started at the mill the same night in June and, early on, we figured out we'd played both football and baseball against each other in high school. That got us talking and we never stopped. He was Polish—stocky and blond, with big hammy hands and legs like tree-trunks—and okay, he was pretty wild. When he wasn't out with one of his numerous girlfriends, he was hanging around the blues clubs in East Chicago and Gary. He was also the only guy I'd ever met who read as much as I did. Or was as big a baseball nut— we argued constantly about that, him being a Yankees fan and me for the White Sox.

Kathy met him one time, in July, when we ran into him at the Big Wheel with one of his girlfriends—and instantly took against him, even though he couldn't have been more polite. But I'd made the mistake of telling her about some of our conversations and she'd already concluded he was a bad influence on me. By which she meant he encouraged me to talk about ideas and try to puzzle out the way things are and not to settle for the boring kind of life most people had.

"Would people say Cassius Clay is full of himself if he were white, if he hadn't announced he was changing his slave name to

Muhammad Ali the day after he trounced Sonny Liston?" Duke would ask, out of the blue. Or, "What if that Tonkin Incident was just trumped-up bullshit, an excuse to bomb the hell out of Vietnam?" And he was obsessed with the Kennedy assassination, convinced that Lee Harvey Oswald hadn't killed the President alone.

"Where were you when you found out?" he asked me one night.

"At the hospital," I said. "With my dad and brother. It was the day after my mom got diagnosed with a brain tumor. Talk about surreal. Sitting in the waiting room, watching it over and over on TV while she was in surgery. She died," I added. "In the spring."

"Jeez. That's awful," Duke said.

I nodded, grateful that he didn't press me to say more.

Every night we took our dinners out to the yard and ate them sitting on rusted oil drums underneath the stars, as far away as we could get from the college boys just there for the summer. "The Eddies" Duke called them, after Eddie Haskell, Beaver Cleaver's brother's ass-kiss friend.

They called Duke "The Polack," but only behind his back.

He called *himself* a Polack, fine—but it really pissed him off if anybody else did and, sure enough, eventually one of them said it loud enough for us to hear across the yard. The other Eddies laughed. Duke jumped up, knocking his lunch pail over, and headed their way. Shit, I thought. He's going to take them all on. He could have, too—and they knew it. It would've been funny the way they looked seeing him coming at them, except I knew that if Duke hit someone he might do real damage. Plus, he'd get fired, and where would that leave me?

I stood, raised my fists. But when he got to where they were all standing, palms out, in anxious surrender, he stopped short, threw up his arms to the smoky sky, and shouted at the top of his lungs, "'...The only people for me are the mad ones, the ones who are mad to live, mad to talk, mad to be saved, desirous of everything at the same time, the ones who never yawn or say a commonplace thing, but burn, burn, burn like the fabulous yellow roman candles exploding like spiders across the stars…'"

Then turned on his heel and headed back toward me, grinning.

"Jesus!" I heard one of the Eddies say. "That guy's frigging insane."

Duke brushed his hands, as if cleaning crumbs from them, and sat back down beside me. "Jack Kerouac," he said. *"On the Road."*

"'Yes, yes, yes,'" I responded. "'Mad drunken Americans in the mighty land.'"

"Whoa!" he said. "You know that book, *too?*"

Suddenly, the few hours I spent alone in Greenwich Village rushed back into me, and the shock of possibility I'd felt that night hit me like a blow. I told Duke about finding the book there and the crazy time afterward, reading and rereading it, all the time thinking about running like hell from the life everyone had planned for me. Then getting slammed by what happened to my mom and Kathy taking care of us all through it—and now she was set on getting married.

"Do you *want* that?" he asked.

The whistle for the end of the dinner break blew before I could answer. Duke closed his Thermos, wrapped up the remains of the huge dinner his mom packed for him, and put them in his metal lunchbox, snapping it closed. I did the same. The Eddies passed us on the way back into the plant, keeping a wide berth.

"Listen, pal," Duke said. "We need to *talk*. What do you say I buy you breakfast when we clock out?"

I said, "Sure. Why not?" Then spent the rest of the shift wishing I'd refused. I didn't want to have to try to explain to Duke Walczek how I felt about marrying Kathy when I couldn't explain it to myself. But when we got to the diner, he didn't even mention it. Just ordered ham and eggs for both of us, flirting with the waitress the whole time, then told me about his wild date the night before, as if this were all the evidence against marriage that anyone could possibly need.

No way was he going to end up like the rest of his family, he told me. "I got four brothers, all of them older than me, all of them butchers—like my old man." He laughed. "They all hate me. Seriously. I'm the demon child: I refuse to go to mass. I refuse to take up the cleaver."

He had tapped the little spiral notebook he kept in his shirt pocket. "I'm going to be a writer," he said. "As soon as I get out of this hellhole and get a life worth writing *about*."

It was his favorite topic of conversation: places he wanted to be instead of here. New York, California, Paris. Maybe even Russia; it would be cool to see what communism was really like. Or Africa— and go big game hunting, like Hemingway did.

Kathy knew none of this. I'd stopped mentioning Duke after that night at the Big Wheel. She didn't know I'd rediscovered *On the Road*, or that Duke had lent me other books, too. Or that he'd gotten me a fake ID and, lately, we'd gone to the clubs in East Chicago after work a couple of times—and that I'd liked it.

"If you're feeling guilty about your girlfriend," Duke said after the first time, "what she doesn't know won't hurt her. And if she finds out?" He grinned. "I'll testify. You fought off those girls at the Cadillac Club and Mr. Archie's like John Wayne taking on the whole Comanche tribe."

"Right," I said. "I'm sure Kathy would think you were totally credible."

I did feel guilty, though. Not because I'd flirted with some girls, not even because, for all intents and purposes, I'd been lying to Kathy by not telling her I'd been hanging out with Duke. What I felt guilty about was how happy I felt in a bar in the early hours of the morning, blues on the jukebox, smoke swirling in the mellow light, the bartender measuring out the drinks.

The anonymous camaraderie of the drinkers, in which I could be anyone I wanted to be.

THREE

ON THE FRIDAY AFTER LABOR Day, I walked out of the mill, saw that it was just barely light, and it occurred to me that it wouldn't be all that long before I'd be driving home in darkness. In the dead of winter, if I hit the sack about the time the sun came up and slept till three-thirty or four in the afternoon, like I'd been doing since I hired on in June, I'd see maybe an hour of daylight.

I was in a foul mood by the time I got home. Pissed off at the whole idea of clocking in for work at eleven every night, clocking out at seven in the morning, so deaf from the roar of the machinery that I had to turn the radio up full blast to be able to hear anything at all. Pissed off at myself because, the truth was, I was kidding myself about eventually going to college; the way things were shaping up, I was going to be working there for the rest of my life—the only difference between now and ten years from now being that in ten years I'd be married, coming home to Kathy and the four kids she'd made up her mind we were going to have instead of coming home to my goddamn brother standing at the open refrigerator drinking out of the milk carton, like I did that morning.

He knew Mom had hated that. It seemed to me he ought not do it, even though she was gone. Which was crazy, I knew. I drank out of the carton myself before she got sick. I got annoyed when she took it from my hands, poured me a glass and handed it to me with this aggrieved expression on her face, like she was so disappointed that I'd turned out to be such a boor.

She'd probably have gotten all teary-eyed to know I didn't do it anymore, because of her, even though how could it really matter?

"Oh, Paul," she'd say. "Honey."

It killed me to think that. I grabbed the carton from Bobby, sloshing milk on the floor.

"Could you please grow up?" I said. "For once, could you not put your frigging cooties all over the milk carton?"

He stepped back, his hands up in surrender. "Hey! What's with you, man?"

The air suddenly went out of me. I was beat, my eyes scratchy with fatigue, and all I wanted was a hot shower and to fall into bed and sleep. Maybe forever.

Bobby followed me down the hall, like a puppy. He stood in the doorway of my bedroom while I unlaced my work boots, peeled off my grimy clothes. He was wearing his football jersey, and I remembered strutting around in mine a year ago, so cocky and cool, like there was nothing in the world that could hurt me.

"You're coming to the game tomorrow night, right?" he asked. "You and Kathy? Because Coach said to tell you to come on down to the locker room before, if you want."

Great, I thought. And join all the other has-beens who show up, reliving their glory days before the team hits the field—guys we used to laugh about.

I planned to stop in, but there was no time to answer, because his ride pulled into the driveway, blasted the horn twice, and he was gone. No sound but the ftzz-ftzz-ftzz of Mrs. Wampler's sprinkler through the open window.

I don't know how long I stood in the shower, hot water streaming down my body. Ten minutes, maybe. Not thinking. Just feeling the water, breathing in the steam. Back in the kitchen, I picked up the box of Wheaties Bobby had left open on the counter, poured some into a bowl, splashed on some milk, sprinkled a little sugar, and chowed down.

Breakfast of frigging champions.

Kathy put me in an even worse mood, just the sound of her chirpy voice, when she called before leaving for her job at the bank, like she did every morning. I hurt her feelings when I asked if she really thought it made any difference whatsoever to me whether she wore a skirt or her new plaid slacks to the game tomorrow night.

"What's *wrong* with you, Paul?" she said.

I didn't answer. Where would I start?

I just made a static-y noise through my teeth, as if the phone had suddenly gone on the fritz, put my finger on the button to break the connection, and left the receiver dangling against the kitchen wall. If she tried to call back, I didn't want to know.

I flipped the TV channels for a while, coming up with nothing but moronic shows that only housewives would watch, which reminded me of dinner at Kathy's house the night before. Mrs. Benson falling all over herself re-filling my plate of meatloaf, making sure I was happy in every possible way in between nagging Mr. Benson to death about chores that, if you listened to her, had to be done ten seconds after dinner was over, or the whole house was going to fall down around us. The sheepish grin Mr. Benson cast my way when she wasn't looking, as if to say get used to it, buddy, a few years from now this will be you.

Meanwhile, Kathy bringing me up to date on the big party she and her mom were planning for her birthday in October, the very thought of which filled me with dread because I'd come to think of it as The Day I Have to Give Kathy an Engagement Ring. Or Not. Worse, finally alone, we got into an argument when "Blowin' in the Wind" came on the radio.

"I just *love* that song," Kathy said.

"You love it," I said. "But you don't listen to it. The truth is, it's saying the same thing as that commercial you don't like."

"It is not," she said.

"Same message, but prettier," I said.

The commercial, which had interrupted the movie we were watching on TV a few nights earlier, started with a little girl standing in a sunny meadow, counting as she picked the petals off a daisy, one-by-one. When she got to nine, her voice was replaced by a man's voice counting backward, as if for a missile launch. The girl looked toward something she saw in the sky until the pupil of her eye blacked out the whole screen. When the voice got to ten, there was a flash and a mushroom cloud, President Johnson's voice speaking over a raging firestorm: "These are the stakes—to make a world in which all of God's children can live, or go into the dark. We must love each other, or we must die." Then the screen went blank except for the white words: "Vote for President Johnson on November 3."

"For example," I said. "'How many times must a cannonball fly before they're forever banned?' What do you think that means? You don't think that's about the stupidity of war?"

"World War II wasn't stupid, Paul."

"I didn't say World War II was stupid. I'm saying what the song says: *War* is stupid. People need to learn to get along. The commercial says it, too."

"The commercial is repulsive," Kathy said.

I shrugged. "It's true, though."

"So what? What's the point in scaring people to death about it?"

"To make them *think?*"

It was same argument we had the first time we saw the commercial and, later, when it was on the news because a lot of people felt the way Kathy did and went apeshit. She gave me the look she'd been giving me all summer when I said any little thing that offended her, like, I know where *that's* coming from.

Meaning Duke Walczek.

Which was more or less true. But I hadn't given her the satisfaction of taking the bait.

I turned the radio on to make myself stop thinking about her, turned it off, then turned it on again—to a Chicago jazz station, thinking that would mellow me out, but the music felt like fingers twitching all over me. I turned it off again. But in the silence, memories came. They always did.

Like Bobby bolting when the surgeon told us that Mom's tumor was malignant, me chasing him down the hospital corridor, finally cornering him at some double doors where a sign said, "Staff Only. Do Not Enter." Bobby slugging me; then, suddenly, he was sobbing—and I had my arms around him, saying, "It's okay, it's okay," just like Mom would have, if she hadn't been the one he was crying about.

How it was like living in *The Twilight Zone* when she was finally gone—as if our house was still our house, just in a whole other universe. Things turning green in the refrigerator, the bathtub all scummy, Bobby's favorite sweater shrunk to the size a seven-year-old could wear because he didn't know he wasn't supposed to put it in the dryer.

Stop, I told myself. You can't think about this goddamn stuff all the time. It's over, there's nothing you can do about it now. I dropped to the floor, did a hundred push-ups in sets of ten, and then willed myself to sleep.

I felt better when I woke up, at least *alive*, and by the time I picked up Kathy that evening, I'd half-convinced myself, again, that it was summer winding down, the realization that we were grown up now, responsible for our own lives just now settling in that had been making us crabby and out of sorts with each other. I said I was sorry for being a jerk that morning. I remembered to tell her how nice she looked—and she did, though it didn't have anything to do with the outfit she'd chosen to wear.

No matter how aggravated I got at her, she always looked beautiful to me. She was small and curvy, with a heart-shaped face and big brown eyes. She had a quiet way about her, she knew who she was and what mattered to her—not like other girls, all silly and loud and changeable, so that you never knew where you stood with them.

Over dinner, we talked about her day at the bank. I told her about Bobby going off this morning all pumped up, wearing his football jersey.

"It's weird not going back to school, isn't it?" she asked.

"Yeah," I said.

"I don't miss it," she said, surprising me. "All that pressure, you know? Studying all the time, cheerleading practice, student council. One stupid bake sale after another. I like working at the bank. I do my job, go out for lunch, come home and have the whole evening for myself." She smiled and slid closer. "For us. It's nice, you know?"

"Sure," I said. "I know."

Both of us fell quiet as I headed toward the place near the river we liked, a run of slow songs on the radio, as if the deejay knew where we were going. I parked in a pocket of overgrown bushes, beneath a huge maple tree, and turned off the engine. The crickets shrieked in the sudden silence, thousands and thousands of them out there, rubbing their wings in a last song of summer.

We moved to the backseat, which seemed made for two people to lie together, cradled in darkness. Time slowed. Kathy loosened my shirt, moved her warm hands along my back, like you might rub a child's back to help him go to sleep, and I felt hypnotized. I wanted her to do this, only this, forever.

Until—I wanted more. And more and more.

And she gave it to me. She gave me her whole self.

Part of me was still at the river with her when I got to the mill an hour later and found Duke waiting for me where we clocked in.

"Hey!" he smacked me in the arm with a folded newspaper. "Paulie. You've got to read this. Right. Now." He opened the paper, cocked his head toward a little filler stuck in down in the bottom corner of the obituary page, and I read: "Sister of Beat Writer Jack Kerouac Dies in Florida." I skimmed to the part where it said the woman was survived by her mother and brother, residents of St. Petersburg, Florida.

"Wild," he said. "Kerouac living in *Florida?*"

"Yeah," I said. "No lie." Though, actually, I'd never thought of Jack Kerouac living *anywhere*. I'd never thought of him as a real person, for that matter. Until this moment, he'd been caught in the pages of *On the Road,* a stoned hipster on a dark highway, the lights of whatever magical city he was heading for spread out in the distance, like stars.

Duke snapped his fingers in front of my face. "Dig it, man! 'The time has come for you and me to go and see the Banana King.'"

I just looked at him.

"The road," he said. "It beckons!"

"Are you crazy?" I said.

"Yeah, *man!*" Duke affected a low, gruff hipster tone of voice. "Craaaazy!"

I headed for our workstation, and he followed, jumping around me, snapping his fingers to music only he could hear—a sight to see in a guy the size of a small bear, which got me laughing. He wouldn't shut up. On breaks, all through supper, he recited his favorite parts of *On the Road,* regaled me with images of palm trees and girls in bikinis.

Kerouac himself, cooler than anyone on earth, *anyone,* welcoming us with open arms—

"Why wouldn't he," Duke said, "Two cool cats like us." And, in spite of myself, I saw the silver ribbon of highway in my mind's eye, the two of us setting out on it.

FOUR

ON SATURDAYS, DAD AND BOBBY went out for burgers and a movie, which they'd been doing since I started at the mill. Kathy had been doing most of our laundry since my mom died—we just didn't get it right ourselves, she said. So she'd come over around the time they left to catch up on it. She'd taken up drinking coffee when she got the job at the bank, so she'd make a pot and drink it at the kitchen table while she waited for the clothes to wash and dry, reading whatever magazine she'd treated herself to on payday.

Then she'd fold everything, making stacks for Bobby, Dad, and me, which she set on our dressers. She kissed me awake when she delivered mine, and slid under the covers with me, still kissing me, until I turned to make love to her. I had to admit that waking up that way—in a bed, the two of us alone, in a quiet house—made me think marriage wouldn't be all bad.

But when Kathy slid into my bed this Saturday, I was in the middle of a dream about Duke and me on the road, and I wanted to go back to sleep, back to the dream. She kissed me again, pressed the length of herself against me. Her cool skin felt good against mine; instinctively, I took her in my arms. I felt myself quicken. But I couldn't shake the dream from my mind.

And, suddenly, that part of my body just stopped working.

Believe me, this had never happened before.

Kathy lay beneath me, naked, her face blank with desire.

"Paul?" she said, when I curled away from her. *"Paul?"* She touched my shoulder, but I shrugged her hand away. "Paul, are you crying?"

I wasn't. But I was breathing hard, trying not to.

"What's the matter?"

The matter was, I'd been kidding myself: I didn't love her anymore. I hadn't since before Mom got sick, since New York, for that matter. I didn't want to marry her. Ever.

A wild mix of rage and sorrow bubbled up inside me. I felt tricked. By Kathy, who even from the beginning probably had sex with me at least partly because of the promise it implied. By Dad, for leaving us alone on Saturday afternoons—didn't he know she'd end up in my bed? Even by Mom, for getting sick and dying, for making me need Kathy just when I'd begun to see that I might not want what she wanted, that I might not want to be with her forever.

The rage drained away, leaving only sorrow—and though I knew the impulse to hold Kathy again was a dangerous one, I turned to her anyway and, for a long time, the two of us lay in the bed I'd slept in since I was a child, tangled in each other's arms. We didn't make love. I didn't want to, but I let Kathy believe it was because I still couldn't.

"Don't worry, Paul. It's okay," she said, like a good wife.

I should have told her right then; instead, I let it fester in me all day so that by the time we got to the game that night, I felt like an engine maxed out in first gear. I made the trip to the locker room and let everybody razz me about how I was one of the old guys now, then climbed up into the stands carrying a bag of popcorn and a couple of Cokes. Along the top row, a bunch of guys were yelling, "Blood! Blood! Blood makes the grass grow," a time-honored tradition among former players, alums, and dateless malcontents. They waved at me to come up and join them, which might have helped me blow off some steam, but Kathy was waving at me, too, and I veered in her direction.

It did not improve my state of mind to see her work friend Judy and Judy's boyfriend Doug sitting beside her. Kathy reminded me that they had gone to the school we were playing tonight. "I forgot to tell you, Judy and I decided to double at work yesterday," she said. "I had to talk them into sitting on our side, though."

I didn't say anything, just looked at her. The last thing I wanted to do was sit through the game with the three of them, the girls talking about Judy's upcoming wedding like they always did, Doug being the green-ass he was. Once the game started, he criticized practically every play we made, like he'd been Mr. Football Hero himself, when I knew he'd never even played the game. It pissed me off for Bobby's sake and made me tired.

At least I don't have to go to work tonight, I told myself. I sat there, shoveling in popcorn, thinking about how after I took Kathy home I could hit the sack like a normal person, sleep as long as I wanted to, and get up when it was still morning.

Pathetic, I thought. *This* is my idea of a something to look forward to now?

The smack of equipment as the plays came down on the field made me miss the way it felt to hit someone, the rush of it, the satisfaction. What could you do in *real* life where it was a good thing, commendable, to hit someone—and as hard as you could, too?

I glanced over to the parents' section, where Dad sat—and it happened again. This time, I remembered Bobby and me escorting Mom out onto the field last year on parents' night, Dad trailing proudly after us. How, heading back to the bleachers when the little ceremony was over, her arms linked in ours, Bobby and I had looked at each other, grinned, and lifted her just enough so that her feet came off the ground.

"Paul! Bobby!" she said. "You boys put me down. I mean it!"

We just laughed. And she couldn't help laughing, too.

Then, six weeks later, helping her to the car the night Dad took her to the hospital, we had held her arms exactly the same way—because, suddenly, her legs didn't work any more.

The roar of the crowd brought me back to the game, everyone rising.

"Paul!" Kathy screamed. "Oh, my gosh! Paul! Look!"

She grabbed my arm and pulled me up beside her to watch Bobby make a long run from the forty-yard line to score. I yelled my head off with everyone else, remembering the feel of running like that, missing it. And started thinking about Duke and me on the road again.

I didn't have any vacation time coming to me yet and I'd never heard of guys taking time off without pay; I didn't even know if they *let* you do that. But sitting there on the bleachers that night, a has-been at eighteen, watching my kid brother bask in the cheers of the crowd, I started cooking up this scheme to take a week off, barrel down to Florida with Duke, find Kerouac, then hit the road for home. Kind of like touching base in Hide and Seek.

I only wanted to see him. If we took off on a Saturday morning right after work and drove straight through, we could be there early the next morning. A famous writer like Kerouac: How hard could it be to find him? Three or four days, tops. It was totally possible.

Later, when Kathy and I were alone, and I casually mentioned that I was thinking about driving down to Florida for a few days—of course, not saying *why*—she sat straight up in the backseat of the car, pulled her sweater down over her bare breasts, and glared at me. "Paul, you can't take time off work to do that!" she said. "It's totally irresponsible."

Like she was my mother, except Mom was never bossy like that. If she didn't want me to do something, she'd figure out a way to talk to me so I'd end up thinking I didn't really want to do whatever it was, anyway. Surprising the hell out of both of us, I said, "Yeah?

Well, I'm going."

"You're not. I mean it. You can't."

"Well, I am."

She gave me this X-ray look. "With who?" she asked. "Because you're not planning to go alone, are you? You're going with Duke Walczek. I *knew* you'd been hanging out with him."

"I have not been hanging out with him," I lied. "For Christ's sake, when would I hang out with *anybody*, working the goddamn third shift? When I'm not there, I'm with you—or I'm sleeping."

She kept looking at me.

Finally, I shrugged. "Okay, I'm going with Duke. So what?"

"Here's what," she said. "You can choose. And if you choose Duke Walczek, don't think I'll be waiting here when you get back. Because I *won't*."

"Fine," I said. "I don't give a shit what you do. I really don't."

She started crying then, which normally would have made me feel guilty. But it didn't this time. It pissed me off, and made me feel cold and mean inside.

We'd never fought over anything important and didn't know how. We both just clammed up after that and, when we got to her house, she got out of the car, slamming the door behind her. She didn't even look back at me.

It was eleven o'clock by then, exactly when I'd be clocking in most nights. I'd been tired before, but I was bug-eyed now. I couldn't have slept if I tried—and I didn't *want* to sleep because I knew I'd wake up in the same stupid life. So I didn't let myself think, just pulled out of Kathy's driveway and headed over to East Chicago to find Duke.

It's weird there, like a city on the moon: rows of gargantuan petroleum tanks, like big space ships, as far as you can see; tall watch towers that look like they were made from an Erector set—and everything surrounded by high cyclone fences, everything in shades of gray, except for dozens of orange flames burning in smoky haloes beneath the dingy sky.

There was a White Castle on Indianapolis Boulevard, where I knew Duke hung out, and that's where I found him, a half-dozen of the greasy little sliders in a pile in front of him and in the booth beside him, a cute Mexican girl with hair ratted a mile high and pale pink lipstick, her head on his shoulder.

He grinned. "Paul Carpetti," he said. "'The one and only indispensible' Paul Carpetti."

"I'm in, man. Let's hit it."

He raised an eyebrow.

"Don't ask," I said.

"No problem. I don't want to know." He turned to the girl. "Paul and I are hitching to Florida," he said. "We're going to find this guy, this writer. Drive us out to Route Thirty?"

Startled, she asked, "You're coming back, though. Right?"

"Absolutely. Yeah."

He kissed her. She sighed.

Ten minutes later, Duke was sneaking into his house to pack a duffel bag with the basics. Then he and the girl, Carmen, followed me home so I could do the same. They parked down the street from my house and waited while I went in through the open window in my bedroom to keep from waking my dad.

I packed some clothes, my copy of *On the Road,* my catcher's mitt and the ball tucked into it. I tucked a snapshot of my mom, laughing, a silly "Happy New Year 1960!" hat perched on her head, into my wallet. I started to take the picture Kathy had taken of all of us in Mom's hospital room the night of the Winter Formal, the last picture of us together: me slicked out in Dad's suit, Bobby in a ratty football jersey, Dad in the plaid wool shirt Mom had bought him for Christmas before she got sick, Mom in the new robe Kathy had helped us pick out for her, her head still bandaged from the surgery. Smiling. Bobby had said something stupid to make us smile. I didn't remember what.

But I put it back. If I took it I also took the memory of Kathy that night, her sparkly red dress and how pretty she looked in it. How after dancing the last dance with her, a slow dance, I couldn't quite let her go and kissed her, right there in front of everyone, and she couldn't help kissing me back and how a little cheer went up all around us.

I lifted my mattress and retrieved the secret stash I had there, not quite a hundred bucks. Between that and the paycheck I cashed yesterday afternoon I'd have plenty to get by for a while. I just scribbled a note and left it on my pillow: *Dad—Taking off on a road trip. I'm okay. Don't worry.*

Then I was out of the window, heading for Carmen's car. I opened the door, tossed my stuff into the backseat and started to climb in after it, but Duke said, "You drive." He grabbed Carmen, setting her on his lap as he slid over to the window on the passenger's side.

I knew right where to go. When we were little, Mom would point to the sign on Indianapolis Boulevard that said "Highway 41" and say, "Do you boys know that if you followed this road and just kept on going, you'd get all the way to Florida?" Then she'd tell us all about what it was like there. Warm, even in the winter! Palm trees and orange groves, the ocean with its waves crashing onto the sandy beach, goofy little birds scurrying along the lacy froth they left at the edge and seagulls swooping and shrieking above. She and Dad had gone there on their honeymoon, and she'd always hoped, someday, we could all go together. But we never did.

I took Indianapolis Boulevard south, through Highland where there were still cars parked at the Blue Top, the car hops in their short skirts still busy clipping trays full of burgers and fries and Cokes onto half-rolled-down windows, toward the place where the lights of the Calumet Region would end and the dark road would roll out before us. Duke and Carmen made out in the seat beside me, which left me listening to the music on the radio: WLS blasting out from the Loop in Chicago—the Beatles, the Animals, the Beach Boys, the Supremes—and I remembered Kathy and me taking the train into Chicago a year or so ago, walking up Michigan Avenue and coming upon the WLS studio. It was so cool, I thought. In the car by the river with Kathy; alone in my room, thinking or dreaming; on the beach on summer afternoons, transistors propped up on blankets all around us: this is where the music begins.

That day, we watched Art Roberts put a record on the turntable, then heard it—"Louie, Louie"—through the speakers on either side of the big picture window. He glanced up, waved, and Kathy did some dance moves that made him grin at her. I laughed. Kathy dancing like that, right on Michigan Avenue! I pulled her close, which made Art Roberts grin at *me*.

It was nuts how happy that dumb little moment made me. A high school kid in love with his girlfriend, wanting her and knowing she wanted me.

But that was a whole other time. Driving Carmen's beater toward the junction of Highways 41 and 30, about to leave my whole life behind me, I felt half like I was in a movie playing myself doing something I'd never *really* do and half like the person I'd been meant to be all along. When I got to the junction, I pulled into a gas station, Duke extricated himself from Carmen, and we got out, grabbed our bags.

"Write me," she said. "Promise."

"Yeah, babe," he said. "You know I will."

One more long, passionate kiss.

"'It's the world,'" he shouted, as she pulled away. "Paulie! 'My God!...It's the world! Think of it! Son-of-a-bitch! Gawd-damn!'"

FIVE

WE WERE WEARING OUR LETTER jackets, even though it was barely chilly. Duke's idea. We'd be more likely to get picked up that way, he said. Who doesn't trust a guy wearing a letter jacket? I guess he was right because we hadn't walked a mile before a Ford Fairlane slowed down, then pulled over. We took off running toward it. The driver, a guy about my dad's age, leaned over, opened the passenger door, and Duke climbed inside. I climbed in back, amid a clutter of sample cases.

"Thanks for picking us up, sir," Duke said.

"Hank," the guy said. "Call me Hank. Where you boys headed?"

"Florida," Duke answered.

"I can take you as far as Evansville," Hank said.

Then he started right in, talking about being in the war.

From what I could tell, guys who fought in World War II either talked about it all the time or they didn't talk about it at all—my dad was among the latter. He'd been a hero in that war, according to my Uncle Johnny, who told Bobby and me that Dad was wounded trying to carry one of his buddies to safety during the Battle of the Bulge. We knew it was true because once, when we were little kids, rooting around Mom and Dad's closet, looking for hidden Christmas presents, we found a shoebox with his medals in it, including the Medal of Honor.

There was also a picture of Dad in uniform before he shipped out, grinning, looking a lot like I did now. He'd married my mom the day after their high school graduation, and enlisted a week after they came back from their honeymoon. There was a packet of letters, too, tied with a blue ribbon, addressed to Mom in Dad's cramped handwriting. We didn't open them. And nosing around in Mom and Dad's room was off-limits, period, so we didn't dare mention that we had found them—or anything else.

Dad wouldn't have told us about the medals, anyway. Like I said, he didn't talk about the war. But after we found that stuff, the war games we played escalated, and we argued more vehemently than ever about who got to be Dad and who had to be the German soldier he hunted down and killed. As I got older, I read everything I could get my hands on about the war. Some books I'd read over and over, like *Thirty Seconds over Tokyo* and *To Hell and Back*, though I had to keep that one hidden because my mom didn't like me reading a book with "Hell" in the title.

Same with *The Naked and the Dead,* which I also discovered last fall—though if Mom had found that one, she'd have been upset by more than the title. Not to mention, *Catch-22*. I wasn't even sure if I should be reading it. I didn't know what to think about that character, Yossarian, faking sickness to get out of flying his required missions, or of the picture the book painted of the Air Force itself. The corruption, the way officers put their men's lives at risk to further their own careers. But I kept reading anyway—and, in the end, it made an absurd, scary kind of sense to me.

I read *All Quiet on the Western Front*, too; then *Hiroshima*—both of which hit me like a Mack truck. The German soldiers seemed as young and wrecked and sad to me as the American soldiers in *Catch-22* and *The Naked and the Dead.* "Bombs away!"

we kids used to shout, zooming around the yard, pretending we were the Air Force dropping the big ones. We had no idea what happened to real people when the bombs hit.

This guy, though—our ride, Hank. "Best time of my life," he said. He'd been stationed in England, he told Duke and me, a master sergeant in charge of supplies on an airbase, so he never saw any action at all, just did his job and hung out with airmen, who were all crazy. On leave, they'd take the train into London, go to the dance halls and listen to Swing. He saw all the greats: Glenn Miller, Benny Goodman, the Dorsey Brothers.

"I love that stuff," Duke said.

Which I knew was a lie.

"I thought all you kids liked was that Top Forty crap."

"I like some of it," Duke said.

"Those Beatles? You listen to them? Boy, I don't see what *that's* all about."

"Girls love them," Duke said. "You know, the hair. Me, I'm more of a Chuck Berry guy. Not that he makes the Top Forty anymore."

Hank glanced back at me. "You like them? The Beatles?"

I started to say that my girlfriend was nuts about the Beatles, then remembered that, as of a few hours ago, I didn't have a girlfriend anymore—and I was struck dumb by the thought. All I could do was shrug.

"Johnny Mercer," Hank said. "Now *there's* a fellow who can write a song." He sang a couple of bars of "In the Cool, Cool, Cool of the Evening." He had a nice baritone, which kind of surprised me. "'Moon River.' That's his. You like it?"

"Yeah, it's a good song," Duke said. "Good for slow-dancing, if you know what I mean."

Hank laughed.

The two of them fell quiet then and there was just sound of the radio tuned to the music they'd been talking about. It was music I knew, the backdrop to my parents' lives, the music from when they were young. I used to hear it on the radio sometimes late at night, after they went to bed. I heard *them*. They were making love, I knew now. But when I was a kid, the sounds they made had seemed like part of the music to me.

Eventually, I conked out for real—and the next thing I knew, we were stopping for gas south of Terre Haute. Hank chatted with the gas station attendant filling the tank, a greasy disheveled guy with dark circles under his eyes who seemed glad for the company. Duke and I got out and stretched, then headed for the restroom, where Duke took out his little spiral notebook and filled up a couple of pages. Probably notes for the Great American Novel he planned to write.

Back in the car, wide-awake now, the road between me and home getting longer and longer, I listened to Hank hold forth about Barry Goldwater: a good businessman, that's what he was, with a businessman's interests at heart. Goddamn unions, full of Reds, everybody knew it, always lobbying to work less for more. People ought to stand on their own two feet, they ought to have to go out and make a buck on commission, like he did. *That* wasn't easy! Why did we think he was still on the road at three in the morning instead of in bed, asleep, with his wife?

We just let him talk. We needed the ride, but I felt bad for not speaking up and saying that Duke and I were members of the United Steelworkers Union ourselves—my dad was, too, and nobody in the world worked harder than he did. Barry Goldwater was a rich man, Dad always said, born rich, and he didn't have any idea about what it was like for people who had to work for a living. Until now, I hadn't even *known* anybody who was planning to vote for Goldwater in November. A couple of the Eddies were twenty-one, maybe they'd vote for him, being college guys and all. But if Goldwater was their man, they'd been smart enough not to mention it when Duke and I were around.

Hank was a decent enough guy, in any case. When we got to Evansville, he drove past his turn-off and dropped us off on the south side of town, where we'd be more likely to pick up another ride.

"You boys be careful," he said, like the dad he was.

We thanked him, watched him make a U-turn and head for home.

"Leg one, Paulie," Duke said.

We shouldered our duffel bags and started walking.

Cornfields stretched out on either side of the road, here and there the shadows of farmhouses dotted the horizon and red lights blinked at the top of radio towers. We passed a football field—Home of the Blue Devils—and it seemed to me like a lifetime since I'd been at the game with Kathy.

It was still dark, but starting to feel like morning. The weeds along the side of the road were beaded with dew, and there was a fresh smell in the air, a country smell I couldn't name. Duke and I walked in silence. I liked being quiet, watching the night drain out of the sky and everything turn gray, then color up.

There was a silvery gray mist off to the west, hovering over the fields, but to the east the sky was blue, the barns red, the corn green, but drying, brown, at the base. A yellow caution light blinked in the distance and, as we approached and I saw there was a truck stop at the junction, I was suddenly starving.

I guess Duke was, too, because he gave me a look and we both took off, running.

Apple pie and ice cream, that's what we had, because it was what Sal Paradise ate pretty much all the way across the country on his first trip west in *On the Road*. It was good, too: the pie freshly baked, hot, the ice cream melting down the sides. We had seconds, then thirds, and the waitress said we might as well buy the whole pie, it was cheaper that way, so we did—polishing it off, dabbing up the crumbs left in the pie pan with our fingers.

SIX

A TRUCKER NAMED BUD TOOK us the next leg, over the Ohio River—silver as a mirror and perfectly still, so that the trees along the riverbank reflected there looked like they were painted on the water—and into Kentucky, where I'd never been before. Except for our senior trip last fall, I'd never been anywhere, except to Chicago for White Sox games and to see the Christmas windows at Marshall Fields, and a couple of times to a cottage my parents rented on a weedy little lake in Michigan. So it kind of thrilled me to see all the horse farms surrounded by what seemed like miles of white split-rail fence and also what Bud told us were tobacco fields, the big leaves drying on racks alongside the road, like the pages of books. The warm air blowing in through the open window smelled like cigarettes.

"Take a whiff." He tapped the pack of Lucky Strikes in his shirt pocket.

He was a talker, Bud. He'd crisscrossed the whole country hauling freight and had something to say about the high times he'd had in every single place he'd ever been. Oregon, Colorado, New Mexico, Texas. You name it. It beat the hell out of hitchhiking, he said. Never knowing how far you were going to get in a day, who you were going to have to put up with to get there, not to mention not knowing where you were going to sleep.

"You got a truck, you got a rolling motel room." He gestured over his shoulder, to a built-in bed between the seat and the back window.

"You'll notice, the wife even made me up some nice throw pillows." He winked. "I'm going to tell you something, boys: In addition to all its other benefits, trucking is the secret to a happy marriage."

"How's that?" Duke asked.

"Simple," Bud said. "You're gone a lot, you see the world. You romance the occasional lady who doesn't expect anything but a nice steak dinner and a few drinks for a roll in the hay. So you come home and find out the wife's gone overboard with the Sears Roebuck catalogue? It's a small price to pay to dodge the nine-to-five grind, coming home to tuna casserole, whiny kids, and mowing the grass every Saturday morning. There's damn good money in it, too—if you can put together enough to get your own rig."

"Yeah?" Duke asked.

Bud nodded. "You bet."

It sounded like a pretty good life, and I started second-guessing myself. What if I just hitchhiked home, told Kathy I'd figured out it was working at the mill that I hated and what I really wanted to do was drive a truck? I could make as much money, maybe even more. Plenty for a nice apartment and—I don't know, sofas, toasters, irons. Whatever she wanted. Eventually, we could afford to buy a house, brick with three bedrooms and a basement, a two-car garage. She might go for it.

But when Bud dropped us at a truck stop a few miles south of Clarksville and pulled into the truckers' parking lot to sleep, Duke shook his head and laughed. "Poor old Bud. He thinks he's got it knocked, but he's just kidding himself. His leash is just longer than most other guys', that's all."

And I was right back to being in a panic at the very thought of getting married because I knew, if you were a decent person, which I still believed I wanted to be, married was married. You couldn't be halfway married any more than you could be halfway dead.

"Paulie," Duke snapped his fingers. "Hey! Paulie!"

"What?"

He gave me this look. "You doing okay, man?"

"Yeah," I said. "I'm doing great."

"You sure?"

"Aside from being hungry, in serious need of a shower, and sick to death of listening to old farts rationalize their lives. Yeah. I'm swell."

But he kept looking at me. "Listen," he said. "You got more to lose than I do. You got a nice girlfriend, if a girlfriend is what you want; you got a nice family. You got troubles to consider—you know, on account of your mom. Me? That's a different story. My old man will probably be tickled pink when he figures out I'm gone—prove to him he was right all along. I couldn't cut it, you know? My mom, she'll go to mass and pray. Then come home and fuss over the old man and boss my brothers and their wives around and bake *krusczyki* for all the bratty little grandkids—and pretty soon forget I'm not there." He held up his hands, as if in surrender. "I'm just saying, I get it if you want to go back."

"I'm not going back," I said.

"Yeah, well, not going back and *not wanting* to go back aren't exactly the same thing, you know? You might want to think about that."

"I *said* I'm not going back."

"Okay, then."

He held out his hand. We shook.

Then headed for the little grocery store inside the truck stop, where we bought a loaf of Wonder bread, a package of salami, a jar of mustard, a bag of potato chips—and fished out four icy Cokes from the barrel near the cash register, two for each of us. There were four tables outside, under some shade trees, just one lone trucker sitting at one, drinking a cup of coffee, listening to the Sox play Cleveland on his transistor radio. We took a table nearby, and Duke made up the all the bread and salami into sandwiches, just like Sal Paradise did in *On the Road*. He tore open the bag of potato chips.

I smeared some mustard on one of the sandwiches with my pocketknife, chowed down—and, no doubt, it was the best salami sandwich I'd ever eaten in my life. The Wonder bread was soft and chewy, the mix of meat and mustard perfect, the salty crunch of potato chips slipped in between the bread and meat so much more satisfying than lettuce would have been. I wolfed down three in a row; the cold prickle of Coke washing them down made my eyes water.

Duke leaned back against the picnic table, gazed up into the blue sky. "Is this the life, or what?" He grinned. "We haven't even missed work yet, you know? Another day, we won't even remember that frigging place."

"No shit," I said.

But it was a lie. I wouldn't forget it. I didn't *want* to forget it: the pounding of the machinery, the mind-numbing repetition of the work, the way my body ached at the end of the shift, the shock of sunlight every morning. If I forgot that, I'd forget the person I was when I worked there, the person I was in serious danger of becoming.

I rummaged in my duffel bag for my baseball mitt and held it up. Duke nodded and took his out, too, and we threw awhile. Easy at first, then testing out our best stuff on each other. Baseball was my game. I was good at it, and the familiar arc of my arm as I threw, the rhythmic slapping of the ball in my glove never failed to calm me.

Afterward, Duke took his notebook from his shirt pocket and started writing. I tossed my duffel to the ground, stretched out, and used it as a pillow. The sun felt good filtering down through the shade trees, dappling my face. My eyes felt heavy. There was a nice little breeze and, lying there, I could hear the whoosh of cars going by, the occasional semi engine cranking up and wheezing out of the gas station onto the highway, the sound of a dog barking in the distance.

And the ballgame, wafting over from the trucker's table. The crackly sound of the radio and the rhythm of the announcer's voice mingling with the ebb and flow of voices in the crowd made me think of lying in bed summer nights listening to White Sox games on my transistor—Bobby in his own room, doing the same thing. How he'd always knock on my wall when they scored and I'd knock back.

We lived and breathed baseball when we were kids. We played Little League from the time we could hold a bat, we played catch with Dad when he came home from work, we played pick-up ball in Joey Bucko's backyard every afternoon. When it rained, we stayed inside and played by way of our baseball cards. It was always the Sox against another team. We'd set up the field and the dugouts on the living room floor, pull a team name out of the cereal bowl we kept them in, flip a coin for who got to be the Sox—then play the lineups, throwing dice to decide the hits and the plays, moving the players' cards around the bases.

Once we actually saw Keegan pitch a no-hitter in the second game of a doubleheader; once Bobby caught a foul ball hit by Minnie Minoso, the Cuban Comet, who smiled up at him and gave him a wave. He still had the ball, on a little stand on top of his dresser.

Then I was remembering going to a Sox game this summer, without Mom. Dad and Bobby and I sitting in the bleachers, not mentioning her, not talking about anything else, either—not even the fact that the Sox were barely in the game that night and lost to the Yankees, who we hated.

I concentrated on the sound of the game on the trucker's radio, making myself remember other, happier times—but they all had Mom in them, and it only made me miss her more.

"Hey, Paulie!"

I opened my eyes and there was Duke standing maybe fifty feet away, in the parking lot, a skinny old colored guy by his side.

"Paulie! Hey, come here! Bring the sandwiches."

I looked toward the picnic table, where there were a couple of sandwiches left in the bread bag. I picked up the bag, went over to where he was standing.

He took the bag and handed it to the colored guy, who bobbed and weaved a pantomime of thanks, eyes darting, all hunched up, trying to look smaller than he already was.

"Paul, this is Gus," Duke said.

I held out my hand, but Gus took a step back, clutching the bag of sandwiches.

"Negroes aren't allowed in the store," Duke said. "They can buy gas, but they can't go in the store. Is that bullshit, or what? So I told Gus here he could have our extra sandwiches, no problem."

"Sure," I said. "Yeah, he can have them."

Gus opened his mouth, nothing came out.

Duke clapped him on the shoulder. "He's going to Nashville. He says he'll take us that far."

Duke was facing the picnic area, but I was facing the gas station, where I could see three guys standing by a red GTO with a decal of the Confederate flag on the back window, watching us. They were older than we were—built, sunburned, maybe construction workers.

"*Duke,*" I said.

"What?"

I tilted my head, just barely.

But he turned around at stared at them. "You're worried about *them?*" he asked.

"I think maybe Gus is worried about them."

Gus nodded. "You boys be putting yourselves in harm's way you be coming with me."

"They're just bullies," Duke said. "I'm not afraid of them." He walked over to the picnic table, got his gear, and headed toward Gus's beat-up '53 Chevy.

What could I do but get my own gear and follow him, Gus trailing behind?

"Hey, Yankee boy," one of the guys hollered as we went past.

The others laughed.

"I guess ya'll don't know how we do things in Tennessee?"

I ignored him. Gus looked scared to death.

"*Hey!*" the guy yelled again. "Nigger lover."

I could have killed Duke for setting us up like this. If we went with Gus—well, who knew what they'd do. If we didn't go with him, Duke and I were in for a fight, big-time—and after they'd kicked our asses, they were likely to follow Gus and pull him over and beat the crap out of him, too, or worse.

I was pretty sure Gus was thinking the same thing. He didn't say anything, though, just darted a glance at me and picked up his pace. Duke got in front, in the passenger's seat; I slid into the back. Gus got in, put the key into the ignition and the Chevy started up with a cough and a rattle. His hands were shaking on the wheel.

He pulled out onto the highway and we went maybe a mile, none of us saying a word. Then there was the roar of the GTO behind us.

"Lord, have mercy," Gus said, his voice trembling.

"Fuckers," Duke said, his fists clenched. "Those motherfuckers." But he looked worried.

I was scared shitless, myself.

Gus kept his hands on the wheel, his eyes on the road. He was going thirty, tops. His lips were moving, but no sound was coming out. I think he was praying.

The GTO tailgated until the other lane was clear; then the driver pulled up right next to us so the guy in the passenger seat and Gus were head-to-head.

He threw a beer can, hard, and it bounced off of the car door. Gus didn't flinch, he didn't even look at them, just kept driving and praying.

"Nigger lovers," the guy in the backseat yelled at Duke and me. "Y'all go home where you belong."

I don't know how long they stayed right beside us. It seemed like forever until a car appeared on the horizon and the GTO had to zoom ahead and clear the lane.

They played with us a while: speeding up, slowing down. Then, finally, I guess they'd had their fun, because the driver floored it and took off. It wasn't until they were out of sight and I blew out a long breath that I realized I'd barely been breathing.

Gus pulled over. "I know you boys be meaning to do me a kindness," he said. "And I thank you for the sandwiches. But you ain't safe with me, hear? Ain't *none* of us safe. Y'all got to get out now and find you a white man to take you the rest of the way."

"Ignorant hillbillies," Duke said, as Gus pulled away. "Truth is, they're just scared maybe colored people will turn out to be smarter than they are. Then where would they be? I've got friends who are colored, guys I've known since grade school. It pisses me off for them, you know? We should've taken those fuckers out. Seriously. We really should have."

"Yeah, right. All *three* of them?"

He shrugged. "Chickenshits. Throwing beer cans at an old man. That's low."

"It was our fault," I said.

"Bullshit. We were the ones doing the right thing."

"Giving him the sandwiches, yeah. But making him give us a ride?"

"We didn't *make* him. Christ, I just wanted him to see that every white person isn't a goddamn bigot. Tell me what's wrong with that."

"It was stupid. You could have gotten him killed. For all we know they'll go back and find him. And don't try to tell me you weren't scared."

"Yeah, I was scared. So what? Hemingway said courage is being scared and doing the right thing, anyway. Did you know that?"

"Hemingway blew his brains out," I said. "What kind of courage is that?"

Duke shrugged. "Well, I'm not sorry we did it," he said.

"Fine," I said. "Just let's not do it again, okay?"

He shrugged again and took off, walking. I let him get a few hundred yards ahead before I followed him, to get some distance between us.

We were in the middle of nowhere, dead corn as bronze as a penny stretching out on either side of the road and nothing on the horizon but a broken-down barn with SEE BEAUTIFUL ROCK CITY peeling off the side of it.

Duke stopped when he got to it and waited for me to catch up. I took my time.

"Who the hell would want to go to that tourist trap?" he said, when I got there.

Like we'd never argued.

"I bet Carmen would," I said. "You can take her there on your honeymoon."

"Chuck you, Farley." Duke laughed and punched me on the arm. "Reminds me of something my brother said to me. He said, 'You fall for some girl and swear you'll go through hell to get her. Then you marry her and you're there.'"

I barely smiled.

"Besides, you're the one who's supposed to be going on a honeymoon," Duke said. "Not me."

"Yeah, well. Not anymore."

The huge wave of relief that washed over me just saying those words set me off running. Duke followed me. He passed me. I caught up and passed him, then in two seconds he elbowed me out of the way and surged ahead. I'd probably slept eight hours since we left, what with constantly drifting off during the conversations Duke carried on with Hank and Bud. Duke claimed he hadn't slept a wink since Thursday; he'd been too wound up to sleep on Friday, after finding the Kerouac story in the newspaper. But if he was feeling the effect of it, you sure couldn't tell.

We stopped, gasping, at the sight of a little motel—neat as a pin: an office, eight units, and a postage-stamp swimming pool shaded by a stand of oak trees, blue and glittering in the last of the afternoon sun. Then took off running again, toward it.

Duke got there before I did, dropped his duffel on the grass, kicked off his shoes, and shouting "Who-hoo," threw himself into the pool. I followed. The two of us wallowed around like a couple of porpoises until an old lady burst from the office and chased us out with a broom.

"You boys scat now," she yelled. *"Scat!"*

We climbed out, shaking the water from our clothes.

"We're real sorry, ma'am," Duke said. "My buddy and me, we just saw the pool and we were so hot from hitchhiking all day and we just—"

"I said, *scat.*" She took a step toward us, broom raised.

And we did.

SEVEN

WE HALF-RAN, HALF-HOPPED ON THE hot asphalt in our bare feet, laughing and swearing, until we got out of sight of the motel and could stop to put our shoes back on. We walked on for the better part of an hour, thumbs out, our clothes drying as we went, and eventually an old boat of a Pontiac careened to a stop a hundred yards in front of us.

It was a bunch of guys who'd just graduated from jump school at Fort Campbell, on leave and heading for Music Row in Nashville. They made room, saying their names—Travis, Don, Kent, and the driver, Ed. Then Travis tossed us each a Budweiser from the cooler on the floor of the front seat.

The cold beer felt good going down. I finished mine, crushed the can, and Travis handed me another one. They were on their last leave before heading for Vietnam, he said.

"Yeah," Don said. "We're fixing to kick their yellow asses."

They looked like they could do it, too. Hard as rock, everything about them pared down for action—even their hair, which was buzzed so close that you could see the shape of their skulls beneath the skin, the vulnerable little hollow at the base of the neck where the spine attached.

"You guys should enlist, join the party," Travis said. "Beats getting drafted, that's for sure. Ending up a grunt."

I was afraid Duke would go into his spiel on Vietnam, how the Domino Theory was bullshit, the Gulf of Tonkin incident nothing but a big scam to crank things up over there, and there was no way he was going to be cannon fodder for asshole politicians who didn't give a damn what happened to real people, no matter what side they were on. He'd head for Canada first.

But he just said, "No thanks, we'll take our chances."

I said nothing at all. I knew I'd be living on borrowed time when I decided to go to work at the mill instead of going to college. I tried not to think about it. I didn't want to think about getting drafted right now.

"So, where are you guys headed?" Travis asked.

"Florida," Duke said. "Beaches, women. Plus, have you guys ever hear of this book, *On the Road*?"

Nobody answered.

"Man, you should read it. Seriously. It's about this guy who just takes off and hitchhikes all over the place. The guy who wrote it lives in Florida now. We're going to find him. He's a beatnik, a real cool head."

"Those guys are commies," said Travis.

"Nah," Duke said. "They're just like you guys. They're cool. They didn't want to get some crap job and have a bunch of kids, so they blew. Seriously, what's the big difference? You guys are jumping out of planes, they're driving like maniacs all over the map." He shrugged, splayed his hands. "You get the girls, too, right?"

Travis grinned then. "Yeah, we get the girls," he said.

Of which there were plenty in Nashville, they all agreed.

We hadn't planned to spend the night there; we hadn't planned *anything*. But the more they talked, the cooler it sounded. They knew of a hotel just off Music Row, where you could get a room cheap. No problem to drop us off there.

"Let's do it, man!" Duke said.

"What the hell," I said. "I'm in."

The hotel lobby smelled like cigarette smoke and other stuff I figured it was better not to try to identify. The guy at the reception desk wore a grimy white shirt and a thin black tie, his hair slicked back in a ducktail. Rooms are five bucks, he said. No liquor. No girls. No loud music. Pay up front.

"Sure," Duke said.

We shelled out the money, got our key, and took the rickety elevator to the fourth floor. The corridor was poorly lit, the red carpet stained and ragged at the edges. The room was tiny, two twin beds crammed into it. The window overlooked an alley.

Duke beamed. "What a dump," he said.

We showered, changed clothes and headed for Tootsies, which the jump guys had told us was the place to be. The front was painted purple, music rolled out through the open front door—a Patsy Cline song belted out by a girl in a cowgirl outfit, framed by the big front window. We grabbed hot dogs from a street vendor, wolfed them down, then flashed our fake IDs and walked inside, where we bought a couple of beers.

The place was packed—apparently, one big happy inebriated family because we hadn't been there ten minutes when a fat red-faced guy waved us over to his table and, before we knew it, refilled our mugs from their pitcher and introduced us to all of his friends. I was done feeling guilty about having a little fun, I decided. Seriously. I was so frigging tired of doing the right thing. Where had it gotten me? Where did it get my mom? Or my dad, for that matter? He was nuts about Mom, he treated her like a queen, and all he got was a broken heart.

I drained my glass of beer, then chugged another—and when the guy's girlfriend grabbed my hand and dragged me off the barstool to dance, I followed. The band played one of those slow, grinding blues songs. Kay-Lynn, her name was, got all over me and

John Wesley and his buddies at the table whooped it up when I came right back at her.

She was a little heavyset, but cute. Kathy was the only girl I'd danced with since junior high—plus, she'd had never danced like *this.* John Wesley kept handing me beers. I kept drinking them. Kay-Lynn had her share, too, and before it was all over we were dancing so wild and dirty that people gathered in a circle to watch us.

"Do it, son," the lead guitar yelled, and everybody laughed.

When the band's set was over and they'd passed the hat, John Wesley invited us to join them for dinner, but Duke said thanks, but no. We were going up to the back bar for a while, then on down Music Row to catch some other acts. We shook hands all round. Kay-Lynn threw her arms around me and kissed me, giving me just the tip of her tongue, which made me so dizzy I thought I might faint.

She winked at me. "Honey, you be good now," she said.

"You're blasted, pal," Duke said when they're gone. "That chick Kay-Lynn, she'd have had you down on the floor in the restaurant, doing the deed, you know? You ought to thank me for saving your ass."

I tried saying, yeah, thanks a *lot,* but the words turned to mush in my mouth. I couldn't walk very well, either. Duke helped me up the stairs to the back bar, where I leaned against a wall near the door Travis had told us the Grand Old Opry stars used, coming into Tootsies after a show. But the only person who came in while I was standing there was a drunk guy who stood in the open doorway for about a minute, with this look on his face like he thought he'd just landed on Mars, and then backed out, into the alley. Duke brought me another beer. I drank it. I had no idea how many I'd had by then. I'd gone from feeling crazy to feeling kind of numb. Every move I made felt like slow motion.

Duke was in pretty much the same shape. We listened to

the band for a while, then lurched downstairs, making our way through wall-to-wall people out to the street. There was a new band in the front window, the skinny singer wearing tight jeans and cowboy boots, a white hat like the Lone Ranger's perched on his head. He was wailing one of those twangy hillbilly songs that sounded like crying. The air was warm and sticky. No breeze. It had grown dark while we were in Tootsies, and my blurred vision made the streetlamps lining Broadway fuzzy, like haloes. Duke started up the street, but I felt rooted there, invisible to the people swarming around me, laughing and talking. I could see him, but couldn't make my feet move to catch up.

Suddenly, I was bent over puking in the street.

A man stopped and put his hand on my shoulder. "You okay, son?" he asked.

"He is *not* okay," the woman with him said. "Honey, you need to sit down on the curb right now. Hear?"

I sat. They sat beside me.

"You are knee-walkin' drunk," she said. "You ever been drunk before?"

I just sat there, my head spinning, trying not to throw up again.

"Welcome to Nashville," the man drawled, and they both laughed—though not unkindly.

I don't know how much time passed, the three of us sitting on the curb, like it was the most natural thing in the world. Maybe it was, there. The couple didn't seem in any big hurry. They had two boys of their own, the woman told me. Good boys, but prone to get themselves in trouble now and then.

"I'd want someone to stop and watch over them," she said. "Like I know your mama would want someone to watch over you."

She put her arm around my shoulders, told her husband to go get me a Coke. "You drink this, baby," she said when he came back. "It'll settle your stomach. You find someplace to sit for a spell."

"If you're smart, you're done for the night," the man said, just as my dad would have.

"I'm definitely done," I said. "Seriously. Thanks for helping me."

And they walked off, hand in hand.

How I could be thirsty after all that beer, I didn't know. But I was. The Coke was icy cold and tasted great, but I only let myself take little sips. I was afraid if I drank it down too fast I'd be sick again. My stomach settled a little, enough to walk up Broadway in Duke's direction, but he was nowhere to be seen. I walked slowly, weaving a little, stopping to look in the window of a souvenir shop or listen to music drifting out from the other honky-tonks. The bars were mostly set up like Tootsies, with a band in the front window. Framed by the open doorways, people writhed in the neon light, looking weirdly like the pictures of hell the nuns showed us in grade school to scare us straight.

There was a phone booth down by the river and, when I saw it, I knew I had to call my dad. So I went in, dialed "0," and placed a collect call before I lost my nerve. Bobby answered, accepted the charges.

"Paul," he said. "Jeez. Where the heck *are* you? Dad's—"

"Never mind," I said. "Let me talk to him."

"Dad, I'm sorry," was the first thing I said when I heard his voice.

"Son," he said. "Are you all right? Where are you?"

"It doesn't matter where I am. The thing is, I—"

"Paul, where *are* you?"

"Tennessee."

He waited, then when I didn't offer any more information, he said, "Kathy thinks you might be with that boy you've gotten to know at work—"

"Duke Walczek. Yeah. I am. We hitchhiked."

"She said you had an argument last night, after the game. Paul, she told me the two of you are planning to get married."

"*She's* planning to get married," I said. "Ever since graduation, that's all she's been talking about."

"And that's why you left?"

"Yeah, that. I don't know. *Everything.*"

Dad sighed, blowing his breath out audibly. I pictured him in the kitchen, his shoulders slumped, trying to figure out what to say next.

When he finally spoke, his voice was wobbly. "I haven't been myself since your mom—"

He paused. He still couldn't say it: *died.*

"I should have realized it was a mistake to let Kathy take care of us the way she did," he went on. "How having her here all the time, doing all she did for us, might—"

"It's *not* your fault," I said. "I should have just told her I wasn't ready to get married. But I tried to convince myself that if we were going to get married eventually, which I figured we would, why *not* now? If I loved her—but I *don't.* That's the real problem, Dad. I don't love Kathy anymore. The truth is I haven't for a long time, maybe since before Mom got sick. I can't even explain why, suddenly, I just couldn't—I can't…"

"You don't have to explain," Dad said. "Or you can explain later, if you want. Look, Paul, if you get on a bus first thing in the morning, there's a good chance you could be home in time to go to work tomorrow night. You're going to have to tell Kathy what you've decided, no matter what. There's no sense losing a good job over it."

"But I don't want the job, either," I said. "I don't know what I want, Dad. I need to figure that out. I can't do that at home. I can't come back, not right now."

"But Paul," he said. "Where are you going?"

I took a deep breath. "Florida," I said, my voice cracking. "I really am okay, Dad. I'll keep in touch. I promise."

Then I rested the receiver back in its cradle before he could talk me into coming home.

EIGHT

Back at our scummy hotel, I took a shower and passed out on the bed. When I woke at eleven the next morning, my head was pounding, my eyes were puffy, my mouth still tasted of vomit. I was starving. Duke had returned some time in the night and was snoring in the bed next to mine. Sunlight knifed across his face when I lifted the tattered window shade.

He groaned. "Paulie. For Christ's sake, put that frigging thing back down."

"I don't feel any better than you do," I said. "But we need to split, man. Get on the road. Remember? Jack waits."

He groaned again, but sat up. "Okay, okay," he said. "What happened to you last night? All of a sudden you were gone. Too bad, man. Because I hooked up with a couple of fine, fine chicks, and you could've had one of them. Both blond, both knockouts." He cupped his hands out from his chest to suggest the size of their breasts. "I shit you not. They were practically fighting over me. I said, 'Girls, girls, we don't have a problem here. There's plenty of me to go around.' Anyway. So the three of us go back to their apartment, I have no idea where it was—some crappy walk-up somewhere. Man, oh, man—"

He got this look on his face, like he was remembering paradise.

I'd figured out pretty much from the start that you always wanted to apply the bullshit factor to whatever Duke said, especially when it had anything to do with girls. So I just let him talk, responding, "Cool!" or "Wow!" every so often, all the while prodding him out of bed and into the shower. He was still talking when we clattered down the stairs into the quiet street.

We walked toward Broadway, where we found a diner with a handful of people in it, all of them looking as hung over as we were.

"Coffee, boys?" the waitress asked, when we sat down at the counter.

"Oh, yeah," Duke said. "Black."

She poured two cups and set them in front of us. She'd been pretty once. Now heavy makeup couldn't quite cover the lines in her face, and her stomach strained against the seams of her pink uniform. Her dark hair, ratted so high you could see right through it, was streaked with gray. Duke talked a mile a minute, telling her about Kerouac and how cool he was and how we were hitchhiking to Florida to find him—flirting with her like she was seventeen, which she ate up, leaning over as close to him as she could pouring a second cup of coffee, calling him, "Baby."

We ordered ham and eggs and pancakes, which we practically inhaled. Duke wrote her a little love note on the back of the bill, and when she came back with our change she slipped us a bag of sandwiches.

"For the road," she said, winking at Duke. "Y'all get to the beach, you think of me." She pointed to the nametag pinned over her heart. "Peggy Ann Kelly. Write my name in the sand."

We promised. She wished us luck, and we were gone.

We walked downtown, as Peggy Ann had suggested, and caught a city bus going south to the edge of town. It was past two and blistering hot by the time we got off and hitchhiked our way back to Route 41. Breakfast had helped, but my headache was holding on like an evil halo. And even though I'd slept like the dead, the headache made me want to keep my eyes closed, which was just as bad as being tired.

We walked backwards, thumbs out, Duke moving on from the girls last night to fantasize about all the girls we were going to meet once we got to Florida. Cars hurtled past, nobody even giving us a glance.

"Assholes," Duke said. "Where's their Christian kindness?"

"Would *you* pick us up?" I asked.

He snorted.

Finally, we got picked up by another trucker, an older guy, maybe in his fifties—Darnell—and all the way to Chattanooga, through the green mountains, I listened to Duke tell him the story of our life on the road. Like two days made a *life*. Plus, the story he was telling was considerably more dramatic than the way things had actually been. In his version, we stood up to the racist guys at the gas station. There was no mention of them following us and scaring us to death.

And, of course, last night's girls. They were twin Elly May Clampetts now. Which got me to wondering, did he pick up those two girls last night, or were they prostitutes? *Were* there two girls? Was there even *one?*

Darnell listened to Duke's stories, now and then glancing toward me with an expression on his face that told me he knew Duke was full of shit and wondered if I was aware of it myself. Past Chattanooga it was getting to be dusk, and he offered to take us home with him to spend the night.

"Y'all do not want to be hitchhiking down through Georgia at night," he said. "Niggers around here have gone plumb crazy."

"I'm not afraid of Negroes," Duke said, stressing the correct pronunciation. "I've got friends back home who are Negroes."

"This ain't the North, son," Darnell said. "I got nothing against them myself—and it ain't so much them you got to worry about, anyway. You know what happened to them friendly white boys in Mississippi this summer, don't you? You want to end up like that?"

Duke shrugged.

But I'd read about shootings and lynchings by the Klan and by the police, too, who were likely to assume that two guys obviously from the North, like Duke and me, had come down to cause trouble, as they saw it. Maybe Duke was just being a writer, blowing smoke about standing up for Gus and putting those guys in their place, but for all I knew he'd actually talked himself into believing it and had it in his mind to do it again.

Darnell repeated his offer. "Ain't got space in the trailer," he said. "But I got a little pup tent I keep up in the yard for my grandsons and y'all can sleep there."

"Thanks," I said. "We'll take you up on that."

Duke glowered at me. He still wasn't speaking to me when we settled into the tent an hour or so later.

"Come on, man," I finally said. "You know it would've been stupid to hitchhike through Georgia at night."

"That's bullshit," he said.

But I knew I was right. Besides, it was nice stretched out in the tent, the door flap rolled open, letting in the cool air and the scent of the woods surrounding Darnell's trailer. The whir of crickets, the chirping of frogs in some distant pond.

I said, "'Suddenly we were stoned with joy to realize that in the darkness all around us was fragrant green grass and the smell of fresh manure and warm waters. We're in the South.'"

Duke laughed, bitterly. "Yeah, in a frigging pup tent in some old geezer's yard."

He turned away, pretended to be asleep—and pretty soon, he was. Darnell had brought us his grandsons' army surplus sleeping bags and a couple of pillows before he went to bed. The boys were nine and eleven, he said, and showed us their school pictures, which he kept in his wallet. Two skinny, freckled kids with buzz cuts and toothy grins. The sleeping bags smelled a little musty, used; the pillows smelled like little kid sweat. When I stretched out the length of the sleeping bag, my foot touched something in the bottom—and I retrieved a cache of baseball cards rubber-banded together.

It was pitch black, but I didn't turn on the flashlight Darnell had left to see what the cards were. The last thing I wanted to do was wake up Duke and get another dose of his crappy attitude. So I just lay there, holding them in my hand, blindsided by the memory of Bobby and me sprawled out on the living room floor, playing our baseball card game when we were in grade school.

I thought about the two of us playing on our high school team last season, too. How Coach Ropac had called me into his office a few weeks after Mom died. He was at his desk when I got there, a chewed-up cigar in his mouth, his head bent over a stat sheet.

"Carpetti," he said, when he looked up and saw me in the doorway. He waved toward the chair in front of his desk, and I sat down on it.

He looked at me, puffed on his cigar a couple times, then said, "I'm real sorry about your mom, son. That's a tough one. You doing okay?"

I don't know why, but his gruff voice saying that just killed me. All I could do was nod.

He puffed some more.

"We need you, Carpetti," he said, finally. "Hart's nowhere near the catcher you are. I got nobody to replace you. You got a good excuse for not showing up at practice," he added, in the same gruff voice. "That's not a problem. But I think it would be good for you to play—Bobby, too. You talk to him. The two of you show up this afternoon, we're good to go."

He nodded toward the door, dismissing me.

I wasn't sure if I had the heart to play, or if I'd be any good if I tried, but I found Bobby and told him I was going home at lunchtime to get our gloves.

"Okay," he said, always the younger brother.

It had been a beautiful, spring-like day—Mom's crocuses just starting to come up in the yard. I walked through the quiet kitchen, to my bedroom. My glove was on the top shelf of my closet, where I'd left it at the end of the summer—saddle-soaped, softened with Vaseline, a ball in the pocket, crisscrossed with rubber bands to hold it in place. I took the rubber bands off, breathed in the smell of the leather. I took the ball out, threw it up and caught it a couple of times, then set it aside, put the glove on, and crouched in the catcher's position. I punched the pocket, like I did waiting for a hit. It felt good. My thighs burned, I was in crap shape—but that felt good, too. Real.

Later, running wind sprints until I felt like my chest was going to burst, throwing until my arm ached—even the punishment of floor burn when I made a bad slide practicing in gym shorts—all these things had felt the same way. Every day after practice, I ran ten circuits around the gym floor, up the stairs to the balcony and around, then down again. It was worth it for the hard plop of the ball landing in my glove, the feel of my mind telling my arm what to do—and my arm doing it. Throw, run, tag. Whatever.

Coach Ropac never said another word about Mom, and he never gave Bobby or me a break because of it, either. He yelled at us when we screwed up, same as anybody. Playing made little pockets of time bearable—hashing over the games gave us something to talk about at the dinner table.

When we weren't playing or talking about playing, I felt like a zombie. Bobby was pretty much living in a state of rage. Everything set him off. Getting up late because he was used to Mom waking him, breaking a glass he was washing and slicing his finger so bad he had to get stitches, flunking a history test that he hadn't been able to concentrate enough to study for. He hadn't taken it out on people, which was good. But he put his fist through the garage wall one day over who knows what; sometimes I heard him slamming things around in his room. Once I saw him stomping around in the back yard after he took out the trash. Just stomping, from one side to another, mud spattering everywhere.

I couldn't talk to him. The few times I tried, he got pissed off at me.

"Bug off," he said. "What do you know?"

So I just let him be.

Dad hadn't been able to help him, either; he wasn't doing that well himself. As far as I knew, hadn't shed a tear from the day Mom's brain tumor was diagnosed until the day she finally died. But in the weeks afterwards, it seemed all he did was cry. Quietly, for the most part. We'd be watching TV and I'd look over at him and see tears streaming down his face. Sometimes I heard him late at night, though, sobbing, and I felt paralyzed. If I went to him, what would I do? So I just lay there and listened, hoping Bobby was sleeping through it in his room next door.

Now, lying in Darnell's tent, the whole story of Mom getting sick and dying unfolded *again*, like a movie in my mind—only it was like I was Bobby, watching it. Watching *me*. He'd watched me since he was a baby, still in his crib: watched me and tried to do whatever I was doing.

Watching me after baseball season was over and all through the summer, he must have wondered what was happening to me, where his real brother had gone. I'd been so wrapped up in myself I hardly thought about him at all. Worse, I'd been crappy to him ever since football practice started in August. I felt sorry for myself every morning when I drove past school and saw the team practicing. Then, about the time I'd finished breakfast and was ready to go to bed, Bobby would come home, all fired up, and take a long shower, singing at the top of his lungs, and it made me furious that he was happy. That he had a life.

Now I'd taken off without even telling him goodbye.

Willfully, I erased all thoughts but this: *Get to Florida. Figure it out from there*. I breathed the thought in and then out, again and again, until I felt my body begin to loosen and, finally, drift toward sleep.

The next morning, Darnell fixed us grits and eggs, and poured us black coffee so strong I swear a spoon could have stood right up in it. There was a picture of his wife over the stove that he said he kept there with the hope that she'd oversee his cooking and maybe even send down some tips from heaven.

"Your cooking tastes great, I said.

"You ain't never had one of Mary Annie's breakfasts," he said. "That's why. Her biscuits—? No doubt about it. The Lord himself took her right from the pearly gates into His kitchen! That's where she's at right now."

The tiny trailer kitchen was full of her: yellow as the sun, with ruffled white curtains and a yellow-and-white checked tablecloth on the dinette table. Embroidered Bible verses in dimestore frames on every available space on the wall.

"Listen," Darnell said, taking up our empty plates and setting them in the sink. "I got to head for Valdosta this morning, pick up a load there, and I'll take you boys along. Ain't too far from there to the state line. Y'all get your gear and we'll be on our way."

There was no arguing with him. Even Duke could see that. But back in the tent, he said, "You know, we don't *have* to do this, Paulie."

"You take the rides as they come," I said. "That's what Jack did."

I grabbed my duffel and headed for the rig, and Duke followed. He sat beside me, sullenly writing in his little notebook—probably about what a drag I'd turned out to be. When we stopped for a break, he headed for the restroom alone, then bought a Coke and a big bag of peanuts and got back to the rig before Darnell or I got there.

Darnell ignored him; actually, he ignored both of us. When

he started up the engine that morning and the radio came on, he turned the volume up, high, which I figured was his way of saying he'd had had his fill of us, he was doing his Christian duty getting us to a safe place, but didn't want to chat.

Fine with me. I didn't want to chat, either.

But I couldn't doze because the awful country music was so loud. By the time he dropped us at an intersection near the factory where he was picking up his load, yesterday's headache was back full-force and I was in as crappy a mood as Duke was in.

"Y'all are about twenty miles from the Florida state line," Darnell called out of the window. "You boys be careful now."

"You boys be careful now," Duke mimicked under his breath, like a six-year-old. He hefted his duffel over his shoulder and set out walking.

I followed, but stayed a body's length behind him because I knew if I caught up, if I said one word to him, we'd drop our gear and get into a fistfight on the side of the road. The only thing up for grabs was who'd land the first punch.

NINE

THEN A RED, '59 THUNDERBIRD pulled over and stopped, but the door was locked when Duke tried to open it. The woman in the driver's seat looked like a movie star. Dark hair tumbling loose and curly past her shoulders, caked-on red lipstick. She hit the button to roll down the window, turned down the radio; then she took off her big, glittery sunglasses.

"Okay, y'all," she said. "Let me look at you."

Duke glanced at me and we stepped back, suddenly in it together again, while she gave us the once-over. She had the longest, blackest eyelashes of anyone I'd ever seen.

"Fake," I heard Kathy's voice say.

"Well, all right," she said, finally, batting those eyelashes at us. "Y'all don't look like axe murderers. Plus, I'm bored half to death driving all by myself. So come on." She reached over and pulled up the lock. "I'm Lorelei. I'm a mermaid at Weeki Wachee, that's where I'm going. I can take you that far."

"Cool," I said, like a moron.

Duke still stood rooted to the highway. I gave him a little punch on the arm and pulled the seat back forward, and he climbed in before he got his wits about him. I slid into the front.

"Y'all got names?" she asked.

"Oh. Paul. That's me." I nodded toward the backseat. "And Duke."

"Duke." She raised an eyebrow. *"Well."*

Then she put her sunglasses back on, shifted the Cruise-O-Matic into drive, and took off.

I settled back into my white leather bucket seat, and took stock of this fortuitous turn of events. I couldn't help smiling. Damn. There we were on the road in a T-Bird with a *mermaid*, for Christ's sake, the radio playing Elvis and Chuck Berry and love songs from the '50s, warm southern air rushing in through the open windows.

Lorelei took a cigarette from the pack tucked into the visor, punched in the cigarette lighter and lit it. Her fingernails were long, painted the same red as her lipstick.

"Y'all looked like you were on the Bataan Death March back there," she said.

"That's because we were nearly *whined* to death by hillbilly music all the way from Chattanooga to Valdosta," Duke said. "We were still getting over it."

Lorelei laughed. "Where y'all headed?"

"You ever heard of Jack Kerouac?" Duke asked. "The writer?"

Lorelei shook her head.

"Well, he lives in St. Petersburg. That's where we're going. To find him."

"Mmmm." Lorelei took a long, thoughtful drag from her cigarette, breathed out the smoke through pursed lips, like a kiss. "Jack—"

"Kerouac. He wrote this book, *On the Road.*"

"And now y'all are on it," she said. "I think that's nice. And I'm going to do my part to get you there as quick as I can."

Was she tweaking us? I couldn't tell. All I know is she floored it and the T-Bird surged ahead, the needle on the speedometer rising. We crossed the state line going ninety. She gave a little wave as we passed the welcome center, with its sign offering free orange juice to travelers.

"Boys," she said. "Welcome to the Sunshine State."

There wasn't much traffic, and we cruised along between eighty and ninety, Lorelei singing along with the radio, low. She was maybe twenty-five; stacked, but thin. She was wearing a tight sleeveless top, open at the neck, a delicate gold cross nestled between her breasts, tight black pedal-pushers that showed off her long legs. And black high heels.

I made myself concentrate on the landscape to keep from staring at her—which was a little disappointing because, so far, Florida looked a lot like every place we'd seen hitchhiking. Crappy little towns, trailer parks, decrepit speedways, sketchy mom-and-pop motels. Old white farmhouses, with cows and horses grazing in the fields; ramshackle churches out in the middle of nowhere, with their messages of hell and damnation; tall water towers with their sloppily painted declarations of love.

There were palm trees, though, mixed in with tall skinny pines. And trees hung with what looked kind of like the angel hair Dad put on our Christmas trees—only it was an ugly gray-brown that made them look spooky. Spanish moss, Lorelei said. There were orange groves, too, and the billboards lining the highway promised the sun-and-surf Florida I imagined.

After we'd been driving awhile, Duke cleared his throat, leaned between the seats. "So. You're a mermaid," he said.

"I am," Lorelei said. "Y'all heard of Mermaid Springs?"

"My mom went there once," I said. "Well, she and my dad went, on their honeymoon. But she's the one who told me about it."

She beamed at me. "Well, then, when we get to Weeki Wachee, you can send her a postcard and tell her you met a real mermaid in Florida."

I opened my mouth, but nothing came out.

Duke leaned between the seats. "She died," he said. "Paul's

mom. Last spring."

"Oh, no," Lorelei reached over and touched my shoulder. "It's a terrible thing to lose your mama when you're young. I know. I like to died *myself* when my own mama passed. It was ten years ago, and I still think about her all the time. And my daddy, well, he was no help to me whatsoever. Honestly. Six months hadn't passed and he up and married this horrible, uppity churchwoman, Dee, who couldn't see the backside of me soon enough. That's where I was, visiting them up near Macon—though I don't know *why* I bother. Believe me, Earl Watson is no longer the daddy I knew.

"'Brenda Marie'—that's my real name, which he *knows* I cannot stand and which I changed when I got the job at Mermaid Springs. *Legally* changed. As far as I'm concerned, it's against the law for him to call me that. Anyway. 'Brenda-Marie,' he's always saying. 'It's time you got yourself a husband and made a Christian life.'

"Well, I'll tell you what. My mama was the best Christian I ever knew, and she loved me to pieces just the way I am. She knew I had a calling from the day they took me to see the mermaids when I was just five years old and I said, 'Mama, I am going to be a mermaid when I grow up.'

"And I am," she said. "I said to Daddy when I left this afternoon, 'I am telling you one last time, I do not need a husband. I do not want one. And I don't need you or that damn Dee to tell me what a Christian life is. I have one, thank you very much—without a bunch of high-handed people in it judging me every time I turn around.'"

She fell quiet—maybe she'd surprised herself saying so much.

"I wish I could have sent my mom that postcard," I said. "You could have autographed it. She'd have gotten a big kick out that."

"I would have, too," Lorelei said. "The one with my own picture on it. They just made it. In fact, I brought some to give to Daddy, but he made me so darn mad I thought, I'll keep these for someone who's going to appreciate them." She opened the console between the seats, took them out and handed them to me. "Here. You boys take them."

"Mermaid Lorelei," the card said. "Mermaid Springs, Florida." The photographer had caught her swimming toward the camera, her hair floating in a dark cloud around her face, her iridescent tail so real that I couldn't help glancing at her legs to make sure they were actually there.

"Whoa," Duke said when I handed one back to him. "This is *fine.*"

Lorelei smiled. "Y'all can send them to your girlfriends."

"I don't have a girlfriend," Duke said.

"I just ditched mine."

"Smart boys," she said. "Y'all just keep the postcards then. A little souvenir. Maybe show them to—what's his name? Your writer?"

"Jack Kerouac," Duke said. "Yeah, we'll definitely show them to Jack. Maybe we'll even bring him up to see your show."

"You do that," she said. "Elvis came a while back, and he just loved it. I had my picture made with him. We all did. He said I looked *exactly* like Ann-Margret."

"Yeah, I can totally see that," Duke said.

He settled himself in the corner of the backseat so Lorelei couldn't see him from the rear-view mirror, but I didn't have to turn around and look at him to know that he had his notebook out, writing away.

When we stopped for gas, the first thing he said to me once Lorelei was out of earshot was, "Jesus, Paulie. Even Kerouac didn't get picked up by a goddamn mermaid."

"See. I told you. Take the rides as they come. If we hadn't gone with Darnell this morning, we wouldn't have been where we were when Lorelei passed by."

It ticked him off. Duke hated to be wrong.

Then, after the three of us had eaten at the diner across the highway, Lorelei tossed me her car keys. "Honey, you drive for a while," she said. "I'm tired." And there we were, me at the wheel of the T-Bird, Lorelei in the passenger seat like she was my girlfriend. Duke in the backseat, steaming.

Lorelei asked me about my mom, and I told her the basics of what happened, but mainly what Mom was like. Maybe, being in the T-Bird, I had cars on my mind because I told her about how Mom finally learned to drive just a year or so before she died and Dad and my Uncle Rich had rebuilt a turquoise Buick for her.

"She kept a little statue of St. Christopher perched on the dashboard for safe travels," I said. "Which, believe me, she needed for the four-way stops. She was always waving other drivers through to be polite, which drove my brother and me crazy—and more than once nearly caused an accident when all the drivers she was being polite to started into the intersection at the same time."

Lorelei laughed.

"Not to mention the fact that she drove so slow that people were always risking their lives to swerve around her. We never teased her, though," I said. "She'd have been crushed. It took her so long to get up the nerve to drive and she got such a kick out of tooling around in her Buick that we just gritted our teeth and prayed."

"That's so sweet," Lorelei said. "I just love how boys are with their mamas. If I ever had kids, which, believe me, I do *not* intend, I'd want boys myself. Girls? I swear, they're just like street cats sometimes the way they act toward each other. My own sister, Jean-Ann, was just *awful* to me from the day I was born. Mama would try to make her be nice, but she wouldn't. Well. She was jealous because I was prettier than her. She still *is* jealous. She gangs up on me with Daddy and Dee. They all think I should be like *her,* with her boring, needle-neck husband and her two bratty kids and her fancy house over by the golf course.

"It is overdone," Lorelei said. "That house. You should see it. *T-a-c-k-y.* Anyway. Boys aren't like that. Y'all get pure mad and have a fistfight and it's over. I don't even like most of the other mermaids, if you want to know the truth. The way they're always backbiting and playing up to Les. He's the owner. Honey, let me tell you, they'd walk right over you in their spike heels if they thought it would get them a lead part. Me? I stay out of all that."

She closed her eyes, sighed. "Makes me tired just to think of it."

Two seconds later, she was fast asleep. In the rearview mirror I could see Duke was sacked out, too. Over the radio, I could hear the low rumble of the V-8. The car had some serious horsepower just waiting to let loose. I gave it a little more gas, turned up the radio, and headed on down the highway, Jerry Lee Lewis screaming, "Goodness, gracious, great balls of fire!"

This wild joy—like nothing I'd ever felt before—rushed into me. I felt different, but utterly myself. Like some new self, one I didn't yet know.

TEN

ABOUT TWENTY MILES OUTSIDE OF Weeki Wachee, she told me to pull over so she could take the wheel. "The car belongs to Les," she said. "Honey, he would kill me if he found out I picked up hitchhikers. Not to mention let you drive."

She stopped again and let us out at a road sign that said:

Weeki Wachee
1 mile

"Y'all walk on in. You'll see Mermaid Springs; you can't miss it. There's not a thing on either side of it for fifteen miles—and it's *pink*. Wait in the little grove across the way while I take the car back to Les. I've got in mind a place where y'all can stay the night."

She gave a little wave and took off, the red taillights with their little horizontal bars disappearing into the darkness.

Duke looked at me, grinned, and we set out after her.

There was a nice breeze that rustled through the pine forests on either side of the road, cooling the humid air and bringing with it the scent of evergreen and water.

The occasional car or truck whooshed by. We probably could have made it to St. Petersburg that night, but neither Duke nor I turned and stuck out our thumb when we heard them approaching. Soon a billboard advertising Mermaid Springs appeared: a gargantuan version of Lorelei swimming toward us in the Florida night.

Duke stopped before it. "'Visit Beautiful Mermaid Springs,'" he read aloud. "'See Real Mermaids Perform Amazing Acts Underwater in Eight Shows a Day.'"

"'Amazing acts,'" he repeated. "Holy shit. Hit me, Paulie. So I know it's real."

I gave him an easy shot in the bicep.

"'Yes, yes, *yes,'*" he murmured, and we walked on until the sprawling pink building came into sight.

It sat close to the road, "Mermaid Springs" spelled out in neon script above it and big posters advertising the shows framed all along the front. The ticket office was dark; the pink concession stand was shuttered. There was a fountain, its spray of water lit by colored lights at the base of a blue concrete pool, and it would have been nice to take off our shoes and cool our feet, but Lorelei had told us to wait in the grove across the street, so Duke and I walked over there, dropped our gear a little way in and sat down, each of us leaning against an orange tree, to wait for her.

We didn't talk, just breathed in the faint scent of the growing oranges mingled with some unfamiliar mix of earth and water. I looked up at the sky—the same sky, the same moon and stars in it that I'd seen all my life, but the sky seemed larger and darker, the moon and stars brighter somehow. I picked up an orange that had fallen from its branch and held it in my hand like a baseball. It was smaller than a baseball, though, and a little shriveled, not shiny, like oranges in the supermarket—not even orange, but washed-out yellow. I was shocked by the sudden intense scent of orange that emerged from it when I broke the skin with my thumbnail. A voice in my head—Sal Paradise's voice—said, clear as anything, "'Adventuring in the crazy American night.'"

If I had repeated the words out loud, Duke would have

assumed I was talking about the craziness of Lorelei picking us up, the two of us in the grove, now, waiting to see what would happen next, when, in fact, the burst of orange made me feel cut loose, like *anything* could happen. I didn't want to try to explain it, so I kept it to myself.

Lorelei had told us that she lived in one of the cottages behind Mermaid Springs and, and after we'd watched for the T-Bird to pull into Mermaid Springs and drop her off for nearly a half hour, Duke said, what if she got dropped off before we got to the grove? Maybe we should sneak around the side of the theater building and see if we could find her.

"Remember Clayton?" I asked. "The night watchman? The guy she told us about at the diner? The *bodybuilder*? Anyway. If she already got dropped off and she's not here by now, there's a good chance that letting us off the way she did was her way of dumping us nicely."

"She's not dumping us," Duke said. Then. "Shit. You think she'd do that?"

"Beats me," I said.

Duke sighed. "Well, let's give it another ten minutes. Then split. If we're lucky, we can still hitch a ride into St. Petersburg tonight."

But not long afterward we heard a rustling behind us, in the grove, and Lorelei appeared, trailed by a girl about our age—blond, wearing a flowered sundress that showed off her curves, pretty in a Kewpie-doll way.

"This is Mermaid Anastasia," Lorelei said.

The girl grinned, rolled her eyes. "I'm Bev," she said. "Call me Bev."

"Bev." Duke stuck out his hand; they shook. "Duke. Pleasure to meet you."

"This here is Paul," Lorelei said.

Bev smiled at me, but stayed right there at Duke's side.

"I was talking to Clayton," Lorelei said. "That's what took so long. Honestly, he is a man who will talk you half to death. First he had to tell me all about his cheating girlfriend, then I had to tell him about Daddy and Dee, and Jean-Ann being so smug and bossy, and work my way up to how I gave you boys a ride. Then he had to give me a little lecture about picking up hitchhikers and I said, 'Clayton, I *know*. But I looked these boys over real good before I let them in the car, and I could tell they'd act like gentlemen.'"

Duke gave a little bow, and Bev giggled.

"He's *always* talking to us girls about how we shouldn't have anything to do with anybody who's not a gentleman," Lorelei went on. "I listened politely, like I always do. I said, 'Clayton, you are so right. We all really do need to be careful—and I promise, I *am*. Then I said to him—" She exaggerated her accent, batted her eyelashes. "'Clayton? Honey? I'd really love to give these nice boys a tour of the theater.'

"Of course, he didn't come right out and say I could. He said, 'I'm about to go out on my rounds, and I'll check on the door.' Meaning he'd leave it open for us."

"He's a peach," Bev said.

"He *is*. Les would kill him if he knew."

"Les would kill *us* if he knew," Bev said.

They laughed.

Lorelei had put on fresh lipstick and some perfume—an earthy scent that was unfamiliar to me, nothing like the flowery perfume Kathy wore. She took my hand and we headed back into the grove. As soon as the picnic area was out of sight, we turned and walked a diagonal path through the woods, toward the highway, which was completely empty, the moonlit road stretching one way, south, to St. Petersburg, and the other, north, toward home.

"Quick, y'all," Lorelei said. "Run."

We did, disappearing ourselves into the pine forest on the other side of the road, Lorelei still in those high heels. We slanted through the trees and eventually came out at the side of the theater, which was built right into the natural spring for which it was named. The spring was about the size of a football field, lined with stone. So deep, Lorelei told us, that the bottom had never been found.

"And clear," Bev added. "The water comes up from the caves under the ground. So do turtles—and all kinds of fish. Catfish, big ones—*ugh*. Sometimes a dozen of them at a time will gather around us—they *love* our sparkly tails—and we have to bonk them with our air hoses to get them away. Once, I kid you not, an alligator swam up from a hole under the theater while one of the girls was in the tank cleaning the glass."

"'I quit!'" were the first words out of her mouth when she got out of the water," Lorelei said. "Well, once she got done screaming. She was cleared out of her cottage in an hour."

We stood, looking at the dark water.

"So you just jump in?" I asked. "In those…tails?"

I felt like an idiot as soon as I said it, but Lorelei just put a finger to her lips and gestured for us to follow her alongside the theater to a door with "NO ADMITTANCE" on it, which opened at her touch. We slipped in and she closed it behind us. There was nothing but metal stairs, lit by a single bare bulb in the ceiling, and we dropped our gear on the landing and walked down to what would have been the basement if there'd been anything above it. It was chilly and dark; it smelled like water. The control room, to our left, with its turntable and microphone, its panel of toggle buttons, looked like a radio studio—except for the window of water that took up one whole end of it.

We walked past, through the dressing room door, into a big room with long counters that had mirrors above them and short stools pulled in beneath, each station marked with a Mermaid's name and cluttered with girl stuff. There were two hairdryers, the kind they had in beauty shops. Costumes and glittery mermaid tails hung on clothes racks. But there were lockers and showers, too—and on the far end, a round, tiled opening in the floor that looked like a sewer.

"*That's* how we go in." Lorelei kicked off her shoes and sat down, locking her legs together at the ankles and dangling them over the opening; then she put her arms behind her and lifted herself to show how it worked. "You just let go and whoosh down the tunnel," she said. "I'm used to it now, but the first few times—"

Bev shuddered. "I'm used to it, too, but I never will like it," she said.

We went from there into the darkened amphitheater, where rows of benches, like church pews, faced a huge window that framed the underwater stage. Lorelei sat on one of them, then took my hand, pulling me down beside her. She kept hold of it as we sat looking at the ghostly scene—the fairytale castle, fish threading through the plants surrounding it, an occasional turtle swimming by. Everything lit by the moonlight that shone from above.

"It's like being an astronaut," Lorelei said. "Being underwater, you know? How you see them on the TV and it looks like they're swimming in air?"

"No gravity," I said.

"No gravity," she repeated. "Like the rules of the world do not apply to you. Sometimes I think if I could just stay down there, if I never, ever had to come up, I'd be so happy."

She looked at me a long time, then ran a finger the length of my face—and kissed me.

Duke and Bev had disappeared by this time, so it was only the two of us when we set out walking hand-in-hand toward the row of mermaid cottages at the edge of the woods behind the theater. Neither of us spoke. There was just the sound of the breeze rustling the trees, the buzzing and whirring of insects. The sound of my heart pounding in my ears. Could Lorelei hear it?

Everything in her tiny cottage was pink. Pink walls, pink linoleum, pink-and-white checked curtains. Pink dishes and coffee cups; pink knick-knacks. Even the cabinets in the tiny kitchenette were painted pink. There was a pink flowered couch and a little TV on a pink table.

Lorelei didn't say a word. She folded back the pink bedspread from her bed in her pink bedroom; she undressed me, kissing every part of my body she revealed. Then pulled me down with her into the bed.

ELEVEN

ONE OF THE LAST TIMES I had sex with Kathy, we went to the drive-in to see *Bikini Beach*. Frankie Avalon and Annette Funicello dithering, as usual, over their relationship and ending up living happily ever after—until next summer, when they'd do it all over again. Kathy talked through the whole movie, which *she* had chosen, so I was watching Frankie and Annette, but hearing her soundtrack: Our Perfect Wedding and Beyond. There was a brand new apartment complex over on Cline Avenue and she had gone to look at it with Judy because Judy and Doug were getting married in October and wanted to rent an apartment before that and have it ready so they could move right in after the honeymoon. It was small, but cozy, Kathy said. Fine until they were ready to have kids.

She got quiet and I thought she was watching the big climactic drag race scene in the movie. But, no. She sighed, happily. "I can't *wait* till we have kids," she said. "Two boys, two girls. A boy first, I think. Troy Dean. I just love that name."

"*Troy Dean?* Are you nuts? He'd be eaten alive on the playground," I said, realizing too late that by making him a "he," I'd made him real.

"Well, what name do you want then?" Kathy asked.

"I don't want any name. I don't want any kids. Not for a long time, anyway. I'm not ready for that."

"For Pete's sake, Paul, I'm not talking about *tomorrow*. I'm talking about—" She waved her arm out, toward our future. "Why do you have to be so crabby every time I talk about—"

"I'm tired, okay? For Christ's sake, I got maybe three hours of sleep this morning."

She sighed, not happily this time. "I hate that stupid third shift," she said. "I really do. How long do you think it will be before you can go to days?"

Like she assumed I was going to be working at the mill forever. She moved right up next to me, did this thing she always did with her tongue in my ear that made me weak, then kissed me—and I kissed her back. "This is a stupid movie," she said. "Let's go, Paul. Let's—" She ran her finger lightly along my thigh.

I removed the speaker box from the window, put the car in gear and drove slowly down the long lane of cars with their steamed-up windows and out into the street, to our place by the river, where we climbed into the backseat and fell into each other's arms. At first, it felt urgent, like it used to. Then, when it was time, when I felt like I couldn't wait one more second, Kathy pulled away.

"Tell me you love me," she said.

"Kath," I said. "For Christ's sake, don't talk. Not now."

"Paul. I need you to tell me you love me."

"Okay. I love you," I said. "I *love* you."

And we went on, but it didn't feel right. We didn't talk on the way to her house. I didn't look at her; I was afraid to, because I was pretty sure she was crying. When we got to her house, she opened the door, got out of the car.

"Kath," I said.

But she closed the door, hurried up the sidewalk.

Maybe if I'd followed her—what? We'd have made up and I'd probably still have been on my best behavior Saturday night, at the football game. Right now I'd be getting home from my shift, getting ready to hit the sack—instead of sitting in Lorelei's pink cottage, drinking the cup of coffee she'd poured before blowing me a kiss and disappearing down the path to get ready for the first show. Where I felt good about having sex, because Lorelei *made* me feel good about it.

"Beautiful boy," she'd said, running her hand along my body. "Look at you."

I hadn't been embarrassed. I'd felt—alive. Like I *was* my body and my body had been made to do whatever pleased me—and Lorelei. I'd never thought sex could be like that: just pure physical pleasure.

Mid-morning, when it was nearly time for the show, I sneaked out and took the path through the woods to the theater, where I picked up the ticket she'd left me at the box office. Watching her perform, her dark hair floating in a cloud around her face, her glittery tail swaying, I half-believed she really *was* a mermaid, and I wanted to keep it that way. I wanted the night we'd spent together in her pink cottage to remain pure: a single amazing experience, uncluttered with the kind of conflicted feelings I knew would come of trying to make it anything else.

Afterward, Lorelei came out, her hair still wet, gave me one last kiss, and introduced me to George, one of the salesmen, who she'd talked into giving us a ride into St. Petersburg. Then she waved and disappeared back into the dressing room. I hoisted my stuff into the backseat of the car—then Duke's. He and Bev were still making out. He finally climbed in beside me, kissing her one last time through the window, promising he'd be back.

"Oh, man," he said, as we pulled away. "Was that a wild night, or what?" He grinned, gave me a little punch on the arm. "So what about Lorelei. Did you two sneak over to good old Lou's and do it in the T-Bird?"

"Like I'd tell you," I said.

If George heard, he didn't comment. He was a middle aged-sales rep for the company that kept the souvenir shop stocked. "Your mermaid salt and pepper shakes," he said, when I asked about it. "Your mermaid spoons and plates and coffee cups. Swizzle sticks. Key chains and charm bracelets. Miniature mermaid tails for the little ones. Everybody wants to take a memory home from Mermaid Springs, or a little something for the folks they left behind.

"In fact, 'Weeki Wachee' is Seminole for 'small gift,'" he went on. "I'll bet you boys didn't know that."

"No, sir," I said. "*I* didn't." And got him talking about the Seminoles to avoid any trouble about Duke and whatever gifts he'd gotten from Bev the night before.

"The Unconquered," Duke said later, walking up the stairs to our room at the Y.M.C.A. "The Seminoles. That's what they call themselves, because you know what? We never did actually conquer them. Plus, when Florida was still part of Spain, slaves used to escape down here and the Seminoles would protect them. Suppose old George knows about that?"

"Beats me," I said. "But thanks for not bringing it up."

"No point," Duke said. "Too many cowboy and Indian movies, you know? Nobody gives a damn about the way it really was."

The trip into St. Petersburg had taken only an hour or so—me listening to George go on and on about the Seminoles, as boring as a history teacher, and Duke writing in his notebook. Now, settling into our room at the Y, he started in on Bev again.

"Eleven on the Duke-O-Meter," he said. "And it only goes to ten. Seriously, man. Those girls in Nashville? Bev was like at least *three* of them all at once. I kid you not."

I ignored him—took my stuff out of my duffel and crammed it into two drawers of the rickety dresser, not daring a glimpse at the snapshot of Mom that I'd brought. The room was gross: two iron beds with lumpy mattresses, a battered wicker table between them with a coconut lamp on it and a Gideon Bible on the shelf beneath. There was a scummy sink in one corner, two threadbare towels on a towel rack. No closet, just hooks on the walls for our jackets and whatever other clothes wouldn't fit into the drawers. No rug, just a plain wood floor, with leftover streaks from once being painted white. No chairs.

"So, Paulie." Duke wiggled his eyebrows. *"Lorelei?"*

"I don't talk about what happens between me and girls."

He snorted. "Right. All two of them?"

Which, I couldn't help it, made me laugh.

"Come on," Duke said. "'What are you thinking, Pops?'"

"I am thinking that Lorelei was amazing. End of story."

"Okay, okay. Good enough." He nodded toward the window, through which we could see a tiny slice of ocean. "Surf's up, man. Let's book."

TWELVE

It was a hot, muggy day, with just a hint of a breeze coming in from the water. There weren't many people on the streets, mostly tourists, like us, and some old people in straw hats, doddering along. Duke and I kept up a good pace, passing them at a clip. It wasn't much of a downtown—a dime store, a department store, a couple of hotels, some restaurants and diners, some clothing stores. But it was clean, with low buildings painted in pastel colors, the sidewalks shaded by awnings and lined with palm trees. Every block or so, you approached what looked like just another building entrance, but when you got to it you'd see that it opened into a long, cool tunnel of shops, a glare of sun at the far end of the stucco passageway. We passed an open-air post office, where people were buying stamps and mailing letters beneath a long arcade.

I thought I was walking toward my first Florida beach—girls in bikinis lounging under striped umbrellas, guys playing volleyball or badminton, kids building sandcastles. But when we got to the water's edge, there was just a long pier with a raggedy strip of sand on either side of it. There were a few sunbathers stretched out on towels, a couple of small speedboats pulled up onto the sand. And more old people, sitting on the benches under the shade trees that dotted the grassy area between the sand and the street.

"What's with the geezers?" Duke said. "Man. We need a Plan B here."

"Right." I say. "After we eat."

We headed toward Jimmy's Crab Shack at the end of the pier, which was packed with more old people—mostly leathery men wearing battered fishing hats. Regulars. You could tell by the way they joked with the waitress and she joked back at them.

We slid into a booth. "We just got into town," Duke said, when she brought us menus. "Hitchhiked from Indiana and headed straight for the beach—or so we *thought*." He grinned and gestured toward the end of the pier. "What's with the sand box out there? Where's the real beach, man?"

She didn't roll her eyes, but she might as well have. "This is Tampa Bay," she said. "The beaches are on a barrier island. St. Pete, Indian Rocks, Madeira, Treasure Island. You can get a bus out there every half hour or so."

"What's the best one?" Duke asked. "Where do *you* go?"

She ignored the question, set the menus in front of us. "Be right back to take your order," she said and went to pick up two plates the cook had just set out.

"Cute chick," Duke said, just loud enough for her to hear. He didn't mean it. I'd seen the girls he went out with, and she was completely not his type.

She was skinny and suntanned, freckles everywhere, with blue eyes the color of the ocean outside the window and short white-blond hair cut in little spikes that framed her face. I got a kick out of watching her zoom up and down the counter, setting down plates of food, refilling coffee cups, scooping ice cream, cutting pieces of pie—all the while shooting the breeze with the old fishermen. She called them by name and knew exactly what each one wanted. Coca-Cola, full up to the brim, *no* ice. Fish and chips, a shrimp cocktail, oysters on the half shell. A double order of fried clams for one guy—along with the promise not to mention it next time he came in with his wife.

"How's that gall bladder?" she asked.

"How was the trip up north for your daughter's wedding?"

"Catch anything worth keeping this morning?"

The old guys chatted away, basking in her attention.

"Where you from?" Duke asked, when she took our orders.

"Here."

"You grew up here?"

She nodded, turned to ask the man in the next booth about his grandson's new puppy.

Duke wouldn't give it up. He introduced himself, then me, when she brought our food. "Hey, you ever heard of Jack Kerouac?" he asked.

She did roll her eyes that time.

"What?" Duke asked.

She just shook her head.

"He's this great writer," Duke said. "He lives here. In St. Petersburg."

"I'm aware of that," she said.

"Well, we're looking for him." Duke nodded toward me. "Paulie and me are. That's why we hitched down here: to find him. On the road, man—like in the book, you know? Like I said, we just got here this morning."

"*And—?*"

Before he could reply, a guy a couple of seats down called, "Hon, could you bring me a little extra mayo?" She slapped our check onto the counter and headed in his direction.

"Jeez," Duke said. "What's *her* problem?"

"Maybe she just doesn't like you," I said. "Though that's hard to imagine."

"Ha," he muttered. "Like she's some prom queen who can afford to turn guys away."

A guy at the counter turned and looked at us.

"Duke," I said, in a low voice. "Buddy. Would you please just shut up and eat before one of these guys has a goddamn heart attack? And, while we're at it, remember why we're *here*? How about if you forget about girls for two minutes and we make a plan."

"I say we ask the waitress about Jack," he said. "He might come in here all the time, for all we know."

"He might. But in case you didn't notice, you totally pissed her off. If she does know anything about him, what do you think the odds are that she's going to tell *us?*"

He looked wounded, then put the smile back on his face and glanced toward the waitress, who was obviously ignoring us.

"Don't even *think* about asking her," I said.

"Okay, all right," he said. "I won't."

"Excellent. Now, *eat*—so we can get the hell out of here."

Back out on the pier, Duke said we needed to go back to the dime store we'd passed so he could buy a supply of Big Chief writing pads and some new pens. Those in hand, he said what we needed next was cigars. To celebrate our arrival in St. Petersburg, to aid us in considering how best to proceed. Kerouac himself had smoked cigars on special occasions, Duke reminded me, and smoking one now would be our small tribute to him. So we stopped at a grungy, hole-in-the wall tobacco shop, where the ancient proprietor with slicked-back gray hair brought out two allegedly genuine Cuban cigars from a secret place behind the green curtain that separated the front of the shop from the back.

"Fidel Castro, he smoke this kind cigar," he said, in heavily accented English, which, of course, sold Duke on the deal. The cigars were five bucks each, but I shelled it out. I still had more than a hundred dollars in my wallet. What did I care?

We walked over to the park, sat on a bench, and lit up. I smoked maybe a quarter of mine before I started feeling light-headed and a little woozy. I dropped it on the ground, stubbed it out with my shoe, then closed my eyes and let the little bit of breeze there was wash over my face until the world stopped spinning.

"Wuss," Duke said. Though he looked a little green at the gills himself, and stubbed his own cigar out not long afterward.

We sat slumped on the bench awhile, taking in the sunshine. Then Duke sat up. He tapped the notebook in his shirt pocket, tapped his head.

"It's all there, ready to be made into the Great American Novel," he said. The main character, Duke himself, was going to be named Jack Bliss, he said—Jack, of course. I was in it, too. Rocco Minetti.

"*Rocco Minetti?*" I said. "That's idiotic. Jesus. Don't name me *that.*"

"Rocco Minetti," Duke repeated, firmly. "My book. My characters. You'll like it just fine when you get famous because of it. Like Kerouac's buddies did."

"Yeah, right," I said.

"You think that won't happen? Hey! Put your money on it, man. It's been 'mutely and beautifully and purely decided.' What I'm going to write in those Big Chiefs, starting today, will make Jack Kerouac look like old news."

"If you think that, how come you're so hot to find him?" I asked.

"To pay homage, man," he said, indignantly. "To stand before him and, you know, get his blessing to carry the torch."

He took out his notebook, waved his free arm to take in the whole park. "And now the true search begins. Look at all these down-and-outs lounging around here, Paulie. Are they not exactly the kind of guys likely to hang out in bars where Jack might go?" He stood up. "Let's see what we can find."

"You go," I said, still aggravated about the stupid name he'd given me. "I'll just stay here and pretend I'm an old coot enjoying the weather."

I watched him saunter over to a guy sitting under a nearby tree. "Hey, man," he said. "I'm wondering. Have you ever heard of Jack Kerouac?"

The guy barely opened his eyes, took one look at Duke, and closed them again.

"Jack Kerouac," Duke repeated. "He's a writer. You ever heard of him?"

Most guys ignored him, a few swore at him.

"I'm a reporter," I heard him say to one. "Yep. Doing a story about the writer, Jack Kerouac. Can you help me?"

He looked surprised when the guy got up and walked away.

You dumb shit, I thought.

He was convinced that if we just kept asking, we'd eventually find someone who'd lead us right to Jack Kerouac's door. We spent the rest of the afternoon wandering around, Duke in reporter mode—though it started seeming to me that he was more interested in seeing how many different kinds of people he could ask about Jack.

An old guy at a bus stop, for example:

"Sir?"

"What? Speak up, young man. I can't hear you."

"Sir?" Duke yelled. "Do you know Jack Kerouac?"

"Jack *who?*"

"Jack Kerouac. The writer. He lives here, in St. Petersburg. Me and my buddy here, we're looking for him."

"Writer. No, I don't know any writers. G.D. Reds, most of them."

Lady in a grocery store:

"Jack Kerouac? No, I don't believe I've ever met him."

"Have you ever heard of *On the Road*? He wrote it."

"Honey, I got six kids. I never go *anywhere*. Even if I had time to read, why would I read a travel book? It would only make me feel bad."

Back at the Y, Duke took out one of the new Big Chiefs and made a big ceremony of opening it, clicking his new ball point pen a couple of times—like checking for bullets in a gun.

"Here goes, Paulie," he said. "Some day you can say you were there when Duke Walczek began *Beat Highway.*"

"Gee," I said. "I can hardly wait. Meanwhile, I'll go see if I can find a map of St. Petersburg."

There was a different guy in the office, and when I asked where I could find a map of the city he handed me one from the stack on his desk.

"Compliments of your Y.M.C.A." he said. He glanced down at the register. "You must be one of the new guys. Room 18? Paul Carpetti, right?"

"Yeah. I am."

"I figured you were Paul," he said. "You don't look like a Duke." I laughed. "You're right about that."

His name was Chuck Reilly. He was a student at Gulf Coast College, he told me—thus, the open textbook on the desk. He had a room here, too, and when his night shift ended he'd go up and sleep a few hours. Then head for class—and the second job he had there, in the library.

I told him about working third shift at the mill all summer, and we commiserated about how weird it was being awake in the middle of the night, how your whole life got out of whack and you got to where you didn't even know what time it was—or what day it was, for that matter—and didn't even care.

"I keep telling myself it's worth it," Chuck said. "I'm halfway through. Journalism. After I get my degree I'm going to spend my whole life watching sports and writing about them. I figure that's worth killing myself over now."

I envied him. It would be nice to know exactly what you wanted to do. To feel like every step you took was a step forward—even though taking it might make you so tired you felt like you were going to die.

"What about you?" Chuck asked. "What brings you to Florida?"

I shrugged. "Not working third shift anymore. Not having a girlfriend anymore."

He laughed. "Head for a beach. Any beach. Sounds like a plan to me."

I didn't mention Kerouac. The fact that Chuck wasn't that much older than I was and had a real plan for his life made our quest to find Kerouac seem pathetic. So I just played tourist and asked him about where things were happening around town.

"Got an ID?"

"Yeah," I said.

"Cool." Chuck took the map back, opened it, and marked some places. The Chatterbox, the Tic Toc Lounge, the Twilight. There was a place called the Shipdeck out at Treasure Island.

And the Wild Boar, if we wanted to hitch into Tampa. That was where a lot of the college kids hung out. He also told me about some cafeterias and diners in St. Petersburg—"St. Pete," he called it—where you could get a good, cheap meal.

"There's a great bookstore," he said. "Haslam's. If you're into that."

"Oh, yeah," I said.

It turned out we like some of the same books. *Catch-22, The Catcher in the Rye.* He was reading this crazy book now, he said, *Cat's Cradle.* He'd lend it to me when he finished it; he'd like to know what I thought.

Just then, Duke appeared, all puffed up: the Great American Novelist.

"Paulie," he said. "Let's get some grub. I'm starving."

I introduced him to Chuck, told him Chuck had been giving me the lay of the land.

He grunted in what passed as a greeting. "Any decent diners

around here?" he asked.

"Bessie's." Chuck folded the map he'd marked up and handed it back to me. "Not exactly the Ritz, but it's nearby. Go out the front door, turn right. Then turn left at the first stoplight. It's down the street a ways. You'll see it. Just don't forget I have to lock the door at midnight."

Duke looked at me, cocked an eyebrow.

"Prick," he said, once we got outside. "Man, you know those guys right off. 'Don't forget, I have to lock the door at midnight.' He probably gave you an earful of that shit. Rules. I am *done* with all that."

"Actually, he probably said it because I'd been asking about night spots. He's a nice guy. He's working nights here, going to college."

Duke snorted. "Figures. College boy."

We walked the rest of the way to the diner in silence. When we got there and the waitress had taken our order, I opened the map and spread it out on the table between us.

"Give me your pen," I said.

He unclipped it from his shirt pocket and handed it over.

I divided the map into eight squares, using the edge of the menu as a ruler.

"Okay." I gave the pen back. "We're not going to get anywhere just wandering around asking people if they know Kerouac. So we're going to walk these areas, street-by-street, talk to people, and make a list of places we think he might go."

"Is this Dudley Do-Right's idea?"

"I didn't tell Chuck we came here to look for Kerouac."

"Good. He'd probably call the F.B.I."

"For Christ's sake," I said. "What's your *problem*? He only told us about the midnight thing so we wouldn't get locked out."

Duke shrugged, started looking around, jotting stuff down in his notebook. Probably details of the diner: the booths with cracked red leather seats, the scuffed floors, the pink neon coffee cup in the window. The smell of coffee and bacon, the grit of sugar not quite cleaned off of our table. The down-and-outs lined up at the counter, nowhere else to go; the pasty, heavyset waitress with big bags under her eyes, old enough to be somebody's grandmother.

He was probably writing down stuff about Chuck, too. When he got to the part in his novel about St. Petersburg, he'd probably work Chuck in, give him some awful name that set him up as a total drag. Milton. Ernie. Floyd.

He could be such a pain in the ass sometimes, so full of himself. But then he left the waitress a five-dollar tip for his two-dollar meal.

"Man, that old lady's a sad case," he said, back out on the street. "Can you imagine living like that?"

THIRTEEN

WE WERE BOTH IN A better mood the next morning, considerably more rational.

We grabbed coffee and a couple of donuts at a little bakery, then checked the book at a nearby phone booth to see if Kerouac was listed. He wasn't, so Duke called information and tried to wheedle the unlisted address out of the operator, who finally just disconnected him.

We'd hit the library, we decided; some of the librarians might actually know him. Plus, it seemed symbolic. So we set out, Duke now and then stopping random people to ask them if they knew Jack, which seemed funny to me this time. I couldn't have said why.

The library was a low pink building, with palm trees surrounding it, nothing like any library I'd ever seen before. But it felt like a library inside: the rich quiet made of millions of words. There were big rooms divided by high arched windows framed in dark wood. The bookshelves and chairs and tables were the same dark color—and the desk where the librarian sat, a gray-haired lady with glasses on a chain around her neck.

I felt grounded for the first time since I left home on Saturday night. I remembered how Mom used to take me and Bobby to the library when we were little, how she'd kneel down with us in the children's section looking through the picture books, deciding which ones we wanted to borrow—and then we'd sit in the grown-up section and look at them while she made her own choices. I remembered how proud she was to take me to get my own library card on my sixth birthday, how proud I was of *myself* when the librarian stamped that first little box on it and wrote down the number of books I'd taken out. How, when I was old enough, I'd ride my bike to the library and then back home again, with the books in the basket on my handlebars.

The librarian looked up. "May I help you boys?"

Duke opened his mouth—

"Could you please tell us where the fiction section is?" I asked.

She directed us to the area behind the arches.

"The books first," I said to Duke. "We need to touch the books first. You're the one who said this was a sacred mission."

"Okay, okay," he said.

But when we looked on the "K" shelf, there were no books by Kerouac there.

"Shit," Duke said. "They're all checked out."

A guy at a nearby table glanced up from the newspaper he was reading. Disheveled, unshaven, not quite clean, he looked a lot like the guys we'd seen in Morris Park the day before. There were others, too, their heads bent over books or newspapers, their dirty green army surplus duffels at their feet—and it occurred to me that whatever had deposited them in this place, rootless, without purpose, might have seemed like a grand adventure at the start.

Suddenly, the grounding I'd felt entering the library dissolved. I headed for the exit so fast I almost knocked over a chair, burst out into the muggy air, and sat down on the library steps, sweat pouring down my face.

"Hey," Duke said catching up with me. "Don't you think we ought to ask the librarian about Jack? He might come in here. If we could get her to look up his library card, we could find out where he lives."

"You ask," I said. "Go ahead. I'll wait out here for you."

I sat with my eyes closed, taking deep breaths until he came back.

"Old bat! She wouldn't tell me anything, just looked over her glasses at me. You know how librarians do. Like if she *did* know Jack, she didn't approve of him. Then went back to her stamping." He looked at me. "Paulie? Are you okay?"

"I guess."

But I wasn't. The day passed, then another, and I kept having that weird feeling I'd had at the library. I'd be doing whatever I was doing and, suddenly, I was floating. Nobody, nowhere. And when I came back, which took maybe a few seconds but seemed like forever, I was sweating and scared—though I didn't know exactly what I was scared *of.*

It didn't go away.

I felt weighed down by a kind of darkness that had descended on me that first day at the library. It let up only in moments when, suddenly, in my mind's eye, I saw my mom, alive, doing little things like cooking or pruning her roses or kissing Dad goodbye in the morning and I felt a rush of pure happiness.

Followed by wild sorrow that shot through my body, every single part of it. Like physical pain, like something breaking inside me. If you had looked at my cells through a microscope, I swear you could have seen its glittering sharp edges. When it went away, I was back in the dark place again.

It made me think about this physics theory we studied last spring. Our teacher, Mr. Switzer, was crazy about the weirdness of quantum physics, and was always saying things like, "Every breath you take contains an atom breathed out by Elvis Presley." Or, "The entire human race would fit in the volume of a sugar cube." Or, "Time travel is not forbidden by the laws of physics." Then one day we got to class and he was so pumped up you'd have thought he was about to give us all keys to brand new Corvettes.

"Okay," he said, when the bell rang. "So. A cat is placed in a sealed box. Attached to the box is an apparatus containing a radioactive atomic nucleus and a canister of poison gas."

"That's *terrible*," one of the girls said.

He raised his hand like a traffic cop. "Never fear. This is just a thought exercise invented by a guy named Shrodinger. No actual cat is going to be sacrificed here."

Everyone laughed.

"Anyway. This apparatus is separated from the cat in such a way that it's impossible for the cat to interfere with it and set up so there's exactly a 50% chance of the nucleus decaying in one hour. If the nucleus decays, it emits a particle that triggers the apparatus, which opens the canister and kills the cat. If the nucleus does not decay, the cat remains alive.

"But here's the really neat thing, here's why the theory matters. According to quantum mechanics, the unobserved nucleus exists partly and simultaneously as both the decayed nucleus *and* the undecayed nucleus…"

He paused. "*Until the box is opened*—at which point the experimenter sees either a decayed nucleus, i.e. a dead cat, or the undecayed nucleus, a live one."

He surveyed us expectantly. "So, what is Shrodinger saying here?" he asked. "What does Shrodinger's Cat tell us?"

Silence.

"I know!" he said, beaming. "It seems impossible! Until the box is opened the cat is *both alive and dead*. Quantum physics tells us that there can be two states at the same time."

He'd gone on to lecture about what this meant in terms of our understanding of the universe, but I couldn't get the box with the cat in it out of my mind and, before I knew it, what I was seeing was Mom's closed casket.

What I wanted to ask Mr. Switzer was, "So according, to Shrodinger's theory, if I hadn't watched my mom die, if they'd closed the lid of the casket before I saw her in it, she'd still be alive, right?"

What I'd like to have been able to ask him now was, "Could you call up Shrodinger and ask him how he explains the fact that someone can be both alive and dead *after* you open the box?"

And, while I was at it, how could I be alive in the "now" and at the same time feel equally, maybe more, alive in the past?

FOURTEEN

OVER THE NEXT COUPLE OF weeks, Duke and I walked the sections I'd marked off on the map, Duke forging ahead in the idiotic Hawaiian shirt and RayBans he'd taken to wearing wherever he went; me tagging along, feeling weirder and weirder every day.

We cruised the bars at night, getting back to the Y just under the wire. I'd fall into bed, exhausted, but Duke would get out the Big Chief and work on *Beat Highway*. He went through one notebook, then another. He was Jack Bliss. I was Rocco Minetti. That's all I knew. Sometimes he'd stop, pen poised, beatific.

"I've got to say, this shit is brilliant, Paulie. Seriously. You won't believe it."

"So let me read it," I'd say.

But he always refused—and I couldn't sneak a peek at what he'd written, either. He kept the Big Chiefs, along with all the little notebooks he'd filled up, in a metal lock box he bought at the dime store and wore the key on a chain around his neck. He slept with the frigging thing under his pillow.

He was so obnoxious sometimes. He knew everything; he had an opinion about everything. Those summer nights, on break at the mill, we discussed things. Mostly, we agreed; sometimes, though, we'd argue in a friendly, spirited way. Now he didn't want to have a discussion, he just wanted to impress whoever he was talking to with what he knew.

At least I'm not getting married, I'd tell myself. That's something to feel good about.

Well, for about two seconds. Because my next thought always was, I also wouldn't be getting married if I'd had the balls to tell Kathy the truth about how I felt. When she started in on the wedding plans, all I'd have had to do—once—was tell her no.

Eventually, we began to catch some trail of Jack, mostly during our nightly cruise of the St. Petersburg bars and pool halls. He'd been seen at the Chatterbox, the Twilite Lounge. Somebody had played pool with him at the Tic Toc. A guy who worked at Haslam's Books told us he came in now and then and moved his books from the bottom shelf where the "K's" were and put them, cover out, at chest level so you couldn't help but see them.

He drank shots with beer chasers, we also found out. Duke kept track of all this in his notebook. He started drinking shots with beer chasers every night, in honor of Jack, until he got so drunk he forgot all about looking for him and started trying to make it with some girl, telling her the increasingly dramatic story about hitchhiking down here—which was my only clue about what the novel he was writing in the Big Chiefs might be like.

He made fun of our first ride—Hank, singing "Moon River"— and mimicked his spiel about how Barry Goldwater was going to save us from the Commies. Duke said, "When he dropped us off, I stood in the middle of the highway and yelled at the top of my lungs, 'Fuck you, old man,' as he drove away."

A flat-out lie.

The old lady who chased us out of the swimming pool now had a shotgun. In Nashville, the girls who (supposedly) picked him up were country-singing sisters with a record coming out next spring. We spent the night in Georgia holed up in a trucker's cab because Duke had created a major racial incident when he saved an old colored guy from getting beat up by a bunch of hillbillies.

You can just imagine what he said about Lorelei and Bev.

I'd just walk away when he started in on that bullshit version of our life on the road. It was kind of ridiculous, really. All the shitty things I'd done by then, and I drew the line at not lying about *that?* But I really couldn't stand to listen to it.

Finally, I quit going to the bars with him at all. I also quit waiting around for him to sleep off his hangover so we could make the rounds of daytime places. I got up, grabbed some breakfast, and headed out on my own. I finished walking the segments I'd marked off on the map that first night, drawing a red line down each street when I got to the end of it, noting any promising places I saw along the way. If I found myself close to Haslam's, I checked in to see where Jack's books were on the shelf. If I was in the neighborhood, I scoped out Al Lang Field, where some of the groundskeepers knew him, and see if maybe he'd been by to talk to them.

At first, I pretended to be a tourist so that people wouldn't be suspicious, then I got into it. I bought a cheap camera and snapped pictures wherever I went—things I knew Mom would have gotten a kick out of if we'd all been able to take the trip to Florida together. Houseplants grown as tall as bushes, orchids growing on tree trunks. Pelicans perching regally on pylons out in the water; fishermen lined up so closely along The Pier that you wondered why their lines weren't constantly tangled together. Old guys playing shuffleboard over by the Coliseum; old ladies with their tanned, wrinkly skin and huge rhinestone sunglasses. And the huge, ancient banyan tree outside the library, like a nightmare tree, its multiple trunks twisting out and up, with a brown curtain of aerial roots that dripped from the high branches, making a cave-like shelter inside.

I carried my mitt and my copy of *On the Road* in a rucksack I bought at the Army Surplus Store, grounding for when I needed to remember who I was—along with a jar of peanut butter, a loaf of bread, and a knife I'd swiped from a diner. When I got hungry, usually about the time it started getting really hot, I headed toward the little lake behind the library—Mirror Lake, it was called. When I got there, having stopped along the way to buy a bottle of milk and maybe a candy bar, I sat down under a shade tree and fixed myself a couple of sandwiches and had a picnic lunch.

There was a high school across the street, and there were always kids outside, eating their lunches, screwing around. Guys tossing a football, girls in groups, talking and laughing. Couples off by themselves. I watched, thinking about how a year ago I was just like them. So full of myself, so cool. In a million years, I couldn't have imagined the series of events that had landed me here, all by myself.

I spent the afternoons in the library, where it was cool and I could sit as long as I wanted to, reading. I read a couple of newspapers cover-to-cover every day, caught up on the sports scores; leafed through magazines that caught my interest. There was a whole section of books about Florida, and I looked up the names of trees, plants, flowers, and birds I'd seen. I pored through books about the ocean, fascinated by the diversity of life beneath the surface, a whole world within itself.

I didn't know what Duke did when he got up. Wrote, I supposed. Sometimes we caught a meal together, but listening to him brag about how drunk he'd been the night before or how many girls he'd laid was about as dead boring as following him around, watching him in action. And he wouldn't lay off Chuck, which pissed me off.

I liked Chuck. Most evenings, I went down to the rec room and watched whatever was on TV until he finished studying, then we'd sit around and shoot the shit, sometimes for hours. By then it was just a week or so before the World Series—the White Sox duking it out for the pennant right up to the wire with the Yankees and

Orioles—and we talked about that. Then the Warren Commission captured our attention.

"No surprise it looks like a whitewash," Chuck said. "KGB, Castro, the Mafia. The CIA. Shit, LBJ might have set it up for all we'll ever know." He shrugged. "A lot of people hated him, you know? My own parents hated him. I actually heard my dad tell someone that the assassination was a blessing. No shit. He seriously believed Satan had sent Kennedy to integrate the schools. Or maybe Kennedy *was* Satan." He rolled his eyes. "He never was quite clear about that. I disagreed, but I kept my mouth shut—about everything. Until last spring when a bunch of protesters showed up when I was standing in line to see a movie. This one colored guy had a sign that said, 'My brother died defending democracy abroad—and for what? Theater segregation?'

"I told my dad about it. He'd been in the war, too, and I said I thought the guy had a damn good point. We got into the first serious argument we ever had over it. He really flipped when I started demonstrating myself. It's the reason I'm putting myself through school, living at the Y."

"My mom was nuts about Kennedy," I said. "Like I told you before, she was in surgery when he was assassinated—and I remember my dad making Bobby and me promise we wouldn't tell her when she woke up. He said she couldn't handle it; she shouldn't have to. But when she came out of surgery, she wasn't herself, she was never really herself again, and the assassination didn't seem to register with her at all. Which, I don't know, I guess was a good thing.

"It didn't register for me, either. I mean, sure, I was upset. It was awful. But it seemed small balanced against what was happening to my mom. To tell the truth, it pissed me off how the whole world just shut down because JFK was dead, all that weeping and wailing, and who besides us even gave a shit about my mom, really? Like her life didn't matter as much as his did.

"I never told this to anyone before," I said.

"I see why," Chuck said. "But it makes perfect sense to me you'd feel that way."

He always seemed to say something that made me feel better, or at least see things in a different way. When I told him about feeling guilty about treating Kathy so badly, he said, "Yeah, well, for what it's worth, I had a girlfriend like that once. I bought the ring, we set the date. I broke up with her in the nicest way I could when I realized I didn't want to go through with it, and she hates me anyway.

"It is what it is," he concluded. "Over—which is a good thing, right? At least good *enough.*"

"Yeah," I said. "Good enough."

If Duke came in while we were talking, he'd head for our room without saying a word—then needle me, if he hadn't passed out by the time I came upstairs.

"How's college boy?"

"What's your merit point count with Dudley Do-Right these days?"

The first time he stayed out past curfew, Chuck and I were watching the late movie in the rec room. He was only five minutes late, and Chuck let him in—but told him he couldn't do it again. He'd lose his job if anyone found out.

Maybe Duke didn't believe this, or maybe he wanted Chuck to refuse to let him in, like this would prove his point about Chuck being a drag. In any case, Chuck hadn't let him in the next time he was late, or any time after that, either. I don't know where Duke slept those nights. If I had asked him, he'd have leered at me, implying he'd been with a girl. Maybe it was true. More likely, he slept on a bench in Morris Park.

"Are you even looking for Jack anymore?" I asked him one night.

"Hey! I'm *living* Jack," he said.

"Yeah, well, you should have saved yourself a trip then," I said.

"You could be a goddamn drunk in East Chicago."

He flipped me the bird. "Get bent, Paulie," he said.

I didn't want what Duke wanted anymore. I wanted a real life.

The thing was, though, for better or worse, *On the Road* had changed me. I shouldn't say this, being a Catholic and all, but I believed that book was holy. A voice in it had spoken to me when I picked it up and read the first few pages in the Greenwich Village bookstore and it kept speaking to me as I read and re-read the book in my hotel room, on tour buses, on a bench near the Washington Monument, while all the others climbed to the top. On the train all the way home. Quiet at first, then louder and louder until Mom got sick and, for a time, it went completely silent. Then Duke had brought it back, spouting off at the Eddies that night at the mill. Afterwards, I began to hear it everywhere: in the roar of the machinery; in Kathy's talk, talk, talk about getting married; in the very rhythm of our bodies making love. But if it hadn't been for Duke's crazy idea to look for Jack Kerouac, it was pretty much a done deal that I would have stayed with her.

I figured I owed him something for that. The two of us had set out on this mission together, and I wanted us to finish it before we parted ways. I still wanted to find Kerouac. Maybe shake his hand and say, "Thanks for *On the Road*. It gave me the guts to try to figure out what I want to be." Maybe not, if it seemed like saying it might embarrass or annoy him.

If I could just see him, it would be like reaching a door. He might open it for me; but if he didn't, the door would be right there in front of me, and eventually I'd figure out a way to open it myself.

FIFTEEN

WHEN CHUCK INVITED ME TO spend a Saturday at the beach at Pass-a-Grille, I jumped at the chance. He'd grown up there, he told me. His friend, Ginny, still lived there—next door to one of the beach motels owned by her mom. We headed out in his old red Crosley convertible, which he kept waxed to a high shine, stopping only to grab a box of chocolate donuts and a couple of cartons of milk, which we devoured along the way. The streets were deserted. The pastel storefronts along Central Avenue looked like a movie set, and the palm trees, which still didn't seem real to me, added to the effect.

It was a beautiful day, another in a long string of beautiful days—sunny, in the low eighties. According to Chuck, early October was the absolute best time of the year to live in Florida. Great weather—and, better yet, the summer vacationers were gone and the snowbirds hadn't begun to arrive yet.

"You think there are old people here now?" he said. "Just wait. A month from now, Highway 19 will be crawling with them, every single one of them driving about ten miles an hour." He grinned. "It's a whole different show on the beach, I'll tell you *that.*"

Chuck turned the radio up loud, pounded his fist on the

steering wheel in time to the music—and when a live recording of Little Stevie Wonder came on, we both sang along. Wailed, really. "Fingertips, Pt. 2." We were pathetic. But, man, it felt so good, zipping along the highway, the sun shining in my face. Even when I'd been happy with Kathy, before Mom got sick and my whole life went to shit, I'd never felt good in quite the same way.

"Heads-up on Ginny," he said as we neared Pass-a-Grille. "Her dad's family has lived here basically forever, so we had the run of the place when we were kids. It was a blast. Her grandparents owned the marina and the general store. They had some motels, too—which Ginny's mom had taken over after her dad died. Drowned in a boating accident, when Ginny was seven. Anyway, there were six boys in the family, so she had all these uncles looking out for her. There were aunts everywhere. I couldn't keep them straight—except for Aunt Leeann, who ran the ice cream shop. I mean, how could it get any better than that? Honest to God, we hardly went inside from March to October. Sometimes we even slept on the beach when we got older.

"Not *together*," he added. "Not that way. I've known Ginny since we were in kindergarten, and she's been my best friend since we were eight. Sleeping with her would be like sleeping with my sister. Plus, believe me, Ginny has no time for anything like that. She's had her whole life mapped out since she was twelve.

"*How* we got to be friends?" he went on. "This will tell you all you need to know. My grandparents were visiting and my grandma got into collecting sand dollars. It's a tourist thing, you know? She'd get up early and go out to the sandbar, where they get stranded by the tide, and put as many as she could find in this string bag she carried with her. Then she'd come back and dump them in a bucket of bleach she kept in the yard. So one day Ginny's riding by on her bike and sees her getting ready to dump in her daily catch, plus she sees all the other sand dollars Grandma's already bleached and has drying on the picnic table—and she skids to a stop and starts yelling, 'Stop! Those sand dollars are alive! You're killing them.'

"You should have seen my grandma," Chuck said. "It was hilarious. This skinny, freckle-faced little girl yelling at this skinny, wrinkly old lady, who kept saying, 'Oh, dear. Oh, *dear.*' She was from Ohio. What did she know? The idea that sand dollars might be alive had never even occurred to her.

"At which point, *she* starts yelling, 'Charles! Charles!'

"And I come running out—like I hadn't been at the screen door all the time, listening.

"'Honey, I need you to help me take the sand dollars back to the water,' she says. "Right now. This little girl—'

"Ginny looks at me. 'What's wrong with you?' she says. 'How come you didn't *tell* her?'"

I laughed. "Accessory to murder," I said.

"Exactly what Ginny would have said, if 'accessory' had been in her vocabulary then. Like I said, she was only eight. Anyway, now I'm in trouble with both of them, and they bully me into going along with this plan to take the possibly-still-alive sand dollars back to the water and then have a funeral for the ones that croaked in the bucket of bleach. This involves burying them on the beach and then building this huge monument out of sand. After which, we have to bow our heads, say a prayer, and sing 'What a Friend We Have in Jesus.'"

I was cracking up by this time, but Chuck held up his hand. "Then Ginny says we have to make a pact to save the sea animals. So we do that, hands raised, serious as a heart attack—and after that, Ginny starts showing up at my house every morning practically at daybreak so we can go do some good deed for…*shrimp*. Or whatever she decides needs saving.

"Shit, she's still doing it. She's majoring in marine biology so she can spend her whole life saving the ocean. She's something else. When Ginny makes up her mind about something, do not get in her way!

"Here we are," Chuck said. "Pass-a-Grille."

We cruised down the main drag—two blocks of pastel houses, small motels, a general store, a diner, and a tavern on one side of the street—and across from them, a wide beach giving way to the ocean. Chuck pulled into a parking spot in front of The Palms, a yellow motel surrounded by palm trees. There was a small pool in the front, with lounge chairs and tables around it, shaded by yellow-and-white striped umbrellas. There was a yellow-and-white striped awning over the little outside bar. When Chuck turned off the engine, I heard Frank Sinatra singing.

There was a girl swimming laps and a couple of people stretched out on the lounges, taking in the sun. There were drinks on the tables next to them, with skewers of fruit and little umbrellas sticking out of them. There was a record player stacked with 45s—and when Frank stopped singing, Dean Martin dropped to the turntable.

"The party starts early at the Palms," Chuck said, as we reached the wrought iron gate.

"Hey!" He opened his arms to the girl who climbed up out of the pool and came barreling toward him. "G! Whoa. You're getting me all wet."

"Tough." She shook herself like a dog and got him even wetter.

"Ginny, this is Paul," Chuck said. "Remember? I told you—"

She turned and looked at me—the waitress Duke pissed off our first day in St. Pete.

"*Shit,*" I said, before I could stop myself.

Ginny burst out laughing.

Chuck looked at her, then at me. "What the—?"

Ginny grinned. "You tell him," she said.

"Well. We—uh..."

Ginny gestured for me to continue.

"We met at the Crab Shack. On the pier."

"And you were with your friend," she said, like she was talking to a kindergartner. "The Duke of Earl."

"Look," I said. "Ginny. I'm really sorry about that day. Duke being such—"

"A dipshit?" she finished for me.

"Yeah. That would be Duke," I said.

She laughed some more, and filled Chuck in on what happened.

"I'm really sorry," I said again. "Seriously. I *am.*"

"What did *you* do?" Ginny asked. "Except be dumb enough to hang out with him. I guess I can forgive you for that. Plus, you got him out of there before one of the old guys decided to try to defend my honor. Which would have been really ugly. So—"

She held out her hand. "Friends?"

"Friends," I said.

We shook, then walked on across to The Palms, where one of the ladies lowered the fan magazine she was reading and pushed her big, rhinestone-studded sunglasses down on her nose to get a look at me. "Welcome to The Palms," she said. "I'm Ginny's mom—Loretta. But everybody calls me Lo."

I wasn't used to calling adults by their first name, my parents didn't approve of it, which on top of the fact that I'd never have picked this woman as Ginny's mom (or anyone's mom, for that matter) made me stand there like a dope—*again*—until I finally worked myself up to at least repeating her name.

"Lo. Uh. Well. Thanks for having me."

I kept standing there like a dope—because I couldn't make myself stop looking at her. A reaction that probably wasn't unusual based on the way both Ginny and Chuck were watching me, clearly amused.

What can I say? Lo was tall and tanned and—*stacked.* She must have been a total knockout when she was younger, and she still looked good. Her dark hair was done up in a beehive. She wore a pair of white short-shorts and a yellow bikini top. Her toenails and long fingernails were painted blood red.

She smiled, slid her sunglasses back in place, fluttered her fingers in a little wave. "You kids have fun at the beach," she said—and went back to reading her magazine.

"Gidget goes Pass-a-Grille," Ginny said, once we were out of earshot. But with affection.

We walked over to the cottage next door to The Palms, where they lived. It was once a double, Ginny said. She and her mom lived in one side, and they rented the other for the season. But it was crowded, just two small bedrooms, and when she was twelve, she had convinced her grandfather to connect the two units by taking out the wall between the two kitchens. So she had what amounted to her own apartment.

"Including my own front door," she said, opening it.

Stepping into the small living room was like stepping into the ocean. The walls were painted that light, but intense blue you see in the shallows—the color of Ginny's eyes. The couch and two directors' chairs were a darker color of ocean blue; the lamps, made from glass jars filled with shells, had white shades draped with blue scarves. There was a big, burbling aquarium on one wall with exotic, multicolored fish swimming around in it. The windows were covered with thick white fishing nets; there were framed drawings of shells on the walls—the kind you see in science books.

"Chambered nautilus, right?" I said, nodding toward the shell on the white wicker coffee table—the only thing, except for the drawings that you might have called a decoration.

"Right," she said. "You don't find them in Florida. My dad fought in the Pacific. He brought it back from there."

I didn't say that Chuck had told me about him dying, or that losing a parent was something we had in common. "Chuck said you really love the ocean."

"There's an understatement," he said. "G, show him the inner sanctum."

Her grandfather had also removed the wall between the

two small bedrooms at her request, Ginny said, and painted the room the color of coral. There was a narrow bed tucked into one corner; a cozy little chair in front of the window, which overlooked the ocean; and a white wicker table next to it, neatly stacked with books. A built-in workspace, with drawers and cabinets above and below, took up one of the longer walls; the other walls were lined with shelves filled with books and shells.

"This is amazing," I said.

"Paul," Chuck said. "I'd cool it if I were you, or she'll have you doing hard labor over at Shell Key—which, believe me, you want to avoid. I got suckered into it once and G had me slogging through the mud flats, collecting dead fiddler crabs. Then she'd get pissed off every time I found one, like I was killing them myself."

"Hey!" Ginny gave him the evil eye.

Chuck raised his hands in surrender.

Ginny was still barefoot, wearing just her swimsuit, a faded red one-piece, the kind lifeguards wear. Kathy would have called her a tomboy—and thought it was strange for a girl to be studying science in college. Kathy, herself, was notable for having been the only student ever excused by our biology teacher Mr. Rasmussen from touching a frog—which he prided himself on having required every single student to do in his thirty-some years of teaching—after, finger poised above her assigned frog, she had burst into tears and fled the lab.

Maybe it was strange. But listening to Ginny name the specimens on her shelves, I couldn't help but be impressed. I tried to impress her back.

"The golden olive is rare, isn't it?" I asked.

She cast me a startled glance. "How do you know that?"

"Library," I said. "I got into reading stuff about the ocean there. I'd never even seen it before I came here. I guess I figured it was like Lake Michigan, only bigger—and with salt and sharks."

Ginny laughed.

"So where *did* you find the golden olive?" I asked.

"Scuba diving. I find all the best ones that way."

One of her older cousins had a scuba shop and took people out diving, she told me. He'd started taking her out when she was fifteen. "Actually, pretty much anything you want to do around here, somebody in my family has a business doing it," she said.

"Yeah, Chuck told me that."

"*That,* he's right about." She grinned. "A couple of them own a small fleet of fishing boats; some for commercial fishing, some to take rich guys out fishing for tarpon. My mom has three other places besides The Palms and you'd think she was Nicky Hilton the way she runs them. I kid you not, Lo is one serious businesswoman when she takes off her bikini. And in case you're wondering why the hell I'm working at the Crab Shack, it's because another one of my uncles—Jimmy—owns it. As in *Jimmy's* Crab Shack. He talked me into doing it while his wife, my Aunt Doris, recovers from surgery."

Chuck and I changed into our swim trunks, and then the three of us hauled coolers, a picnic basket full of food, hibachis, blankets, umbrellas, beach chairs, a collapsible table, sand buckets, fishing poles, a volleyball net, a football, a portable radio, and various other necessities across the street and staked out the territory across from The Palms. People started arriving soon after, dragging more stuff. Carl, Linda, Suzie, Brad and Karen from high school—Brad and Karen, obviously a couple. Rick, who Chuck knew from working summers on the beach at Treasure Island. Mary Claire, who volunteered with Ginny on Shell Key. And more, whose names I couldn't remember.

It looked like a small village by the time we got settled: bright beach umbrellas circling the hibachis, weirdly reminiscent of Conestoga wagons surrounding a campfire. A patchwork of different-colored towels dotted the sand. Chuck and I played catch for a while; then a bunch of us played volleyball, at which—no surprise—Ginny was fearsome. I'd never met a girl like her before—always moving, completely focused on whatever she was doing, whether it was making the killer serve or positioning a beach umbrella to allow just the right amount of sun. She seemed to know every single thing about everyone there. I watched from the blanket, where I'd collapsed to soak up some sun, as she checked in on the details of their lives just like she'd done with the old guys at the Crab Shack.

"So, Paul," she said, dropping to her knees beside me when it was my turn. "Did you guys ever find Jack Kerouac?"

"Nah," I said, blushing. "That was Duke's idea. It was really just an excuse to—"

"Take off for the beach?"

"Yeah. Something like that."

She laughed. "Think you'll stay in St. Pete?"

"I don't know," I said. "I like it here. Maybe."

She hopped up at the sound of one of the girls calling her name, started to walk toward her then stopped and looked back at me. "Uncle Jimmy has a tendency to go through dishwashers," she said. "Especially now—with Aunt Doris out of commission. He's kind of a terror, but if you ever want a job..."

"Thanks," I said. "I'll let you know."

I watched her go, then stretched out on the blanket, my eyes closed, breathing in the sunshine, the smell of the ocean and suntan lotion and hotdogs cooking, the sound of laughter and waves crashing into the shore and who knew how many transistor radios all cranked up, all tuned to the Top Forty.

Happy.

SIXTEEN

CHUCK WAS OFF THAT NIGHT, so we stayed for dinner at The Palms, watched the sunset, then hung out playing cards with a couple of Ginny's uncles. I dozed off more than once on the drive back to St. Pete, and I was more than ready to hit the rack when we got to the Y. But when I opened the door to our room, Duke was waiting for me.

"Where have you *been*?" he asked.

"Beach. With Chuck."

"All fucking day? Christ, it's almost eleven."

"How would you know how long I've been gone? What are you even doing here at this time of night? I figured you'd be out."

"I *was* out. I came back to get you. Paulie, listen. I heard a couple of guys talking about Jack—some pool game at the Tic Toc he lost and there's a rematch tonight. This could be it, man. Come on. We need to go. *Now*. I'm serious."

He was hopping around the room like he did the day he showed me the article about Jack being in Florida. He's starting to look like one of those guys who hang out in Morris Park, I thought. His hair was shaggy, he hadn't shaved in a couple of days, he was wearing a pair of jeans and a tee-shirt that hadn't been washed for weeks. He'd been drinking; I could smell it on his breath.

"Come on." He opened the door. He'd started smoking, and he pulled a cigarette from the crumpled pack in his shirt pocket and held it between his twitching fingers, waiting to light it the second we stepped outside. "Let's split, man. Let's make the scene."

"Okay, okay." I followed him downstairs, past Chuck, who gave me a puzzled glance, and out into the night.

There was no pool game going on when we got to the Tic Toc, just a bunch of people hanging out at the bar, all of them three sheets to the wind, listening as well as drunk people can to this older guy who was totally smashed rant about the sorry mess our country had become. He was graying, unshaven, wearing this ratty plaid flannel shirt and baggy, unpressed pants that barely fit over his beer gut.

The Red conspiracy. The *real* Mafia: the Jews. Degenerates.

The guy chugged a beer, followed it with a shot, and struck the empty shot glass on the bar, like a gavel. "You think LBJ can fix any of this, you're sadly mistaken." He waved his lit cigarette, trailing ashes. "He doesn't even want to fix it. The Great Society," he sneered. "Give it all away to the niggers and commie bums who refuse to work for a living. That's his plan. Well, he can kiss my ass."

He slid off the bar stool, bent over to stick up his rear end in case anyone wanted to take advantage of the opportunity, and toppled into the arms of one of the guys at the bar, who laughed and propped him back up, then stayed close so he wouldn't fall over again.

Duke raised the glass of beer the bartender had just set before him. "Yeah," he said. "Let's give it all to the rich, instead. Bomb anybody who doesn't agree with us into oblivion, keep the Negroes in their place. What true-blue American wouldn't vote for that?"

It got real quiet.

"You're a punk," the drunk guy said.

"Maybe." Duke shrugged. "I've read the Constitution, though.

Maybe you ought to give it a go yourself, send it on to the G-man when you're done—not that it will matter in the end. LBJ is going to trounce his ass."

The drunk lunged off of his stool and stumbled toward Duke, his fists up, a lit cigarette dangling between his fingers.

"Whoa! Take it easy." The guy who'd propped him back at the bar grabbed his arm, but the drunk struggled away and lunged for Duke again—who just stood there, fists raised, that little smile on his face that said, "Hey, come get me."

"Duke," I said. "Come on, man. The guy's loaded. Let's get out of here."

But Duke held his ground. Standing next to him was like standing next to a downed electrical wire; I could feel the tension humming through him. Fortunately, the drunk passed out mid-lunge, and his friend caught him again, this time maneuvering him into a booth, where he slumped over, his head on his chest.

"Asshole," Duke muttered.

The drunk's friend turned to him "Hey, fucker. You're the idiot stick who's been running all around town looking for Jack Kerouac. Am I right? Well, congratulations." He nodded toward the booth. "You just found him. Now why don't you and your buddy get the hell out of here before I beat the shit out of both of you."

I'd never seen Duke speechless before, but he was speechless now. Me, too.

This was Jack Kerouac?

"Move," Jack's friend said.

I couldn't move.

Duke didn't move, for whatever reason.

The next thing I knew, a bunch of guys were dragging us out into the parking lot and roughing us up. One of them pushed me hard, and I fell, skidding across the asphalt. I just lay there, my hands raised in surrender. There were way too many of them to make it a fair fight. Duke fought back, though, until one bruiser of a guy got him by the shoulders and pushed him backward over the hood of a car.

"Listen, dumbfuck," he said. "The last thing in the world Jack needs is shitheels like you giving him grief. You found him. Now leave him the hell alone. I see you sniffing around him again—"

He cocked his head, raised a fist. Then yanked Duke up and shoved him out onto the street. The guy who had helped Jack in the bar yanked me up from the pavement and gave me a push in the same direction.

"Get the hell out of here," he yelled. "Both of you."

And they all disappeared back into the Tic Toc.

Duke started walking, muttering under his breath. The more he muttered, the faster he went—until we were practically running. We got all the way to Morris Park, where he collapsed onto a park bench.

I was exhausted, a little sunburned—not to mention the fact that most of my right arm was bloody and burned like hell where I'd scraped it on the asphalt. All I wanted to do was go back to the Y and fall into bed. But it was after midnight, so that was out of the question. Chuck probably would have let me in if I asked him, but then I'd have had to explain what a fucking fool I'd been.

It served me right, anyway, stuck out here with all the losers—which, if I were honest, I was well on the road to becoming myself. They were tucked away under trees and in the shelter of bushes, covered with army blankets or tattered quilts, their arms around beat-up duffels or grocery bags that held all their worldly belongings, embracing them like lovers. It was a cool, clear night, the black sky sprinkled with the same stars that had shone above Kathy and me in those terrible months, lying together in the backseat of the car, when the only thing I wanted, the only thing that could make me forget about my mom for a little while, was the comfort of her warm, living body close to mine, the whisper of her breath mingled with my own.

"Maybe that wasn't really him," Duke said, after a while. "You know what, Paulie? I'll bet it wasn't. I'll bet those guys were just yanking our chains. There's no way Kerouac would be like that."

"Like what? Crazy? Old? In case you haven't figured it out yet, we were never looking for the real Kerouac, we were looking for some idea of him we got from reading the book. But if you think about it, even *that* guy was falling down drunk and crazy most of the time. And that was—when? The forties, the early fifties? That guy was Jack, all right. It just never occurred to us he'd be like that."

"Asshole." Duke stood up, his fists clenched, as if Kerouac were lunging toward him again, as if he'd turned out to be a pathetic drunk for no other reason in the world than to disillusion Duke Walczek, from East Chicago, Indiana, who'd taken to the road to find him.

"This place is shit," Duke said. "Fucking old people. It's depressing. Man, it's time to split this scene. Greenwich Village. Malibu. You name it, Paulie—we're gone." He took out his wallet and fingered the money inside. "I've still got almost a hundred bucks. How about you?"

I reached for my back pocket. It was half-ripped off; my wallet was gone.

"Those *fuckers*," Duke said.

"I don't think they stole it," I said. "They were just pissed about Jack. It probably fell out when that guy threw me in the street."

"You're too frigging nice, Paulie." Duke gave a harsh laugh. "Besides, even if it did fall out, I'd bet my ass one of those guys found it and the bunch of them are drinking on your money right now. We need to go back there and get it."

I looked at him. Jesus. He was spoiling for another fight.

"I'm not going back there tonight," I said. "We don't even know for sure my wallet's there; it might have fallen out while we were walking. If it did, we'd never find it in the dark."

"All right, then. We'll backtrack as soon as it gets light," Duke said. "But if we don't find it, if it's not at the Tic Toc, I've got enough for both of us. Seriously, man. We need to get *out* of here. What do you think? New York? California? New Orleans?"

I want to go home, is what I thought. But when I closed my eyes and pictured home I saw Mom and Dad and Bobby and me there together, and it made me feel so sad, so lost and alone, that it was all I could do not to lie down on the park bench and curl up like a baby. I'd put that picture of Mom in the goofy New Year's hat, laughing, in my wallet, I remembered, which made me feel even worse.

Duke rattled on. "We don't have to hitchhike. We can take the bus, if you want. We don't even have to decide where we're going. We can take the first one out heading any direction. That would be cool, really. We could end up anywhere."

By this time, my teeth were chattering; my skin felt like it was on fire. I couldn't see the ocean from where we sat, but I felt its presence, blacker than the night, stretching all the way to the other side of the world. The fishy scent of the breeze coming in off the water made me feel like I was going to vomit, and I hunched over, my forearms on my knees, my hands dangling. But nothing came. Just this awful heaving.

At which point, Duke finally shut up. "Paulie," he said. "Jeez. What's the matter?"

I raised my hands, blew out a long breath.

"Hey, it's okay about the money. Seriously. I've got plenty."

"It's not the money."

Duke looked at me. "You want to go back, don't you? You want to go home."

"I can't go home," I said.

"Yeah, you can." He sat down beside me. "Look, Paulie, I told you before, home means nothing to me. I got nothing there. But it's different for you. You got your dad and your brother. You don't have to go back with Kathy." He punched me lightly on the arm. "Hey, she probably wouldn't go back even if you wanted her to."

When I didn't laugh, he added, "Or maybe you *want* to go back with Kathy. That's cool, too. If it's what you want."

"I do *not* want to go back with Kathy."

"Okay," Duke said. "Then—"

"I don't know *then*. That's the problem."

"Paulie," he said. "You *choose* what then is. New York, California. Shit. *Dubuque, Iowa*. You name it. I go where you go, *kemosabe.*"

"I can't just *choose,*" I said.

"Yeah," he said. "You can. You have to. *Not* choosing is just another kind of choice, you know?" He looked at me, his eyes narrowed. "Or maybe you already did choose. Maybe you decided to stick around here and hang out on the beach with Dudley—"

Before he could finish the sentence, I was up, my fists raised. "Fuck you," I said. "Chuck hasn't done a goddamn thing to you, so would you please get off my back about him? Just because he's not out getting smashed every night like you are—"

"Pipe down, for Christ's sake," called a voice from under one of the trees. "We're trying to get some sleep here."

"Yeah, knock it off," called another.

We did. We sat back down, but didn't look at each other.

"Okay, okay," Duke finally said, in a low voice. "I'm a shithead. I know that."

"Yeah," I said. "You are." But smiled, in spite of myself.

"I mean it, Paulie. The truth is, my cocked-up idea of hitting the road to find Kerouac was just an excuse to get the hell out of East Chicago. I never should have talked you into it."

"Hey," I said. "I came to East Chicago looking for *you* that night. If it weren't for your sorry ass, I'd be engaged to Kathy by now, picking out my tux for the wedding. So if you're thinking I'm sorry I left, don't. And don't feel like you have to stick around here on account of me, either. It's okay. I know you're ready to move on."

We sat there on the park bench in the cool night air, men with wrecked lives and broken dreams sleeping all around us.

Then Duke asked, "But what are you going to do?"

I shrugged. "Get some kind of shit job for a while. I just need enough to get by until I can get my head on straight. I'll be fine."

"You sure?"

I nodded.

"Okay, then."

Suddenly, I was so tired I couldn't keep my eyes open, my head kept dropping to my chest, and I had that half-nauseous, half-delicious feeling I used to get sometimes when I got sleepy during class, but didn't dare give into it. I got off the bench and lay down on the grass.

"I'm beat," I said. "I need to cop some Z's before we do *anything.*"

"No shit, man." Duke stretched out on the bench, folding his arms so that his hands made a pillow beneath his head. "It's kind of perfect, you know? Tonight? Ending up here? It's something that could've happened in *On the Road.*"

Probably, knowing Duke, he said more. But I fell asleep.

Back at the Y the next morning, we showered and shaved. Duke packed his duffel. We had some apple pie and ice cream at a diner near the bus station, for old time's sake.

"I've been thinking," he said, setting down his coffee cup. "Last night? Kerouac? Man, I do *not* want to end up like him, spewing that kind of crap."

I nodded in agreement.

"California is where things are happening," Duke said. "Berkeley, man. That's where I want to be." He tapped the notebook in his shirt pocket. "Maybe tell a new story."

Who knows, I thought. Maybe he will.

We walked over to the Trailways station, where it turned out there was a bus leaving in ten minutes for Atlanta. He bought a ticket for it, figuring he'd head west from there.

"Well, this is it, pal," he said.

We shook, and he slipped me a twenty-dollar bill.

"In case you don't find your wallet, man."

Then he was through the gate, boarding the bus. He turned when he got to the top of the steps. "So long, Paulie," he yelled. "It was real."

SEVENTEEN

I HADN'T SEEN MUCH OF Duke the past few weeks. Sometimes I'd even wished him out of my life. But when the bus pulled away and it hit me that he was really gone, all I could think about was those long summer nights in the factory, the two of us saving each other from the killing boredom of the place. Right now, he was probably taking the Big Chief out of his duffel and settling in to write the end of our story—Jack Bliss off on the next adventure, this time to save the world, leaving the hapless Rocco Minetti behind to patch together a life.

The stupid name irritated me, again, but at the same time I felt weirdly unbalanced knowing that Rocco would be banished from his imagination as he moved on to the next story. Who was I without Duke to imagine me into a new life?

Who was I without my wallet? If I had to prove I was Paul Carpetti, I couldn't do it, which was scary enough without the realization that having no ID also meant I didn't have to *be* Paul Carpetti anymore, if I didn't want to be—which got me moving, feeling like a balloon that had been blown up and set wild.

I walked randomly for a long time, up one street and down another, not noticing anything until I found myself back at Morris

Park, where my mind cranked into panic at the sight of the bums who'd been chased from their sleeping places at sunrise and had returned to sit on the benches, smoking, reading newspapers or battered paperbacks, the trappings of their portable lives sitting at their feet.

I'd have prayed, if prayer made sense to me anymore. But all I could think of was Mom with her rosary beads, her bald head bent, whispering prayer after prayer asking God to make her better—and He didn't. Why would He help *me* now?

I headed for the library, thinking it would calm me down. But when I got there, I couldn't sit still. I took a book about the ocean from the shelf, leafed through it, set it aside, and got another one. Before long, I had a whole stack of them on the table beside me, the sight of them which so overwhelmed me that I went from not being able to sit still to sitting slumped in my chair, staring at a picture of a live sea scallop with its two rows of beady little eyes.

My whole body ached from the roughing up I'd gotten the night before; I could feel my pulse in the long nasty scrape on my arm. My eyes felt scratchy inside, and I had to fight not to close them. Sleeping was not allowed in the library. The last thing I wanted to do was risk getting kicked out of the one place that felt even a little bit like home to me, so I left and went back to the Y, where I slept like the dead until Chuck knocked on my door around five.

"I'm thinking about going to a movie," he said, when I opened it. "You want—" He stepped back. "Jesus, Paul. What happened to you?"

"Long story," I said.

"Involving Duke?"

"Yep."

"Figures," he said. "Short version, *then* a movie?"

"There's no short version to anything that Duke's involved in."

Chuck sat down on what had been Duke's bed. "Okay, hit me with it," he said.

I still hadn't told him that Duke and I had been looking for Jack Kerouac, I was too embarrassed, but now I told him the whole story—from finding *On the Road* in Greenwich Village to getting to know Duke at the mill—the Eddies, how Kathy hated him at first sight, how he showed up at work that night with the newspaper story about Kerouac's sister's death, the two of us ditching our jobs to find him down here.

"Which we did," I said. "Last night. At the Tic Toc. He was drunk, spouting all this prejudiced crap—though we didn't know it was him at the time—and Duke got pissed and went off. Then Kerouac's friends threw us out of the bar. Literally. Plus, somewhere along the line, I lost my goddamn wallet. It was pathetic. We ended up sleeping in Morris Park."

"So where's Duke now?" he asked.

"He took off for California this morning."

Chuck shook his head. "Everyone knows you guys were looking for Kerouac, by the way. Want to know something funny? Duke didn't ask me about Kerouac because he figured, being the square I am, what would I know about someone like that, right?"

I had to admit it was true.

Chuck grinned. "Well, I know Jack. He's a friend of mine," he said.

"You know Jack?" I asked.

"Yeah. He's a baseball fanatic, and I sat next to him at a Cards game during last year's spring training. We struck up a conversation, somehow got to talking about being into baseball when we were kids and I told him how I'd made up this game I played with baseball cards and dice. It took up the whole floor of my room. I made dugouts from shoeboxes; the bases were potholders. I kept stats. I wrote a sports column after every game. I still have the notebooks. I'd play for hours at a time, giving a running commentary on the game. It drove my mom crazy. She'd make me go outside, but I'd set the whole thing up in the driveway and play there."

"We played a version of that, too. Me and my brother."

"So did Kerouac," Chuck said. "Only, being Kerouac, he made up his own *league*, he invented backgrounds for all the players, kept stats. He also made up a baseball newspaper, where he analyzed the games. He still has all this stuff. I gave him a ride home from the ballpark that day, and he showed it to me. Believe me, it's not as simple as just throwing dice. He's got this wild system of scoring based on years of hitting statistics. It's amazing. I go over and play with him sometimes. It keeps his mind off things."

Chuck paused. "Well, you saw him. He drinks way too much; most of the time he's either pissed off or sad. People drive him nuts. No kidding, I was over there one time and this whole gang of guys showed up on their motorcycles, all of them wearing jackets with "Dharma Bums" on the back, wanting to take him for a ride."

He shook his head. "The thing is, if he ever really was the guy in *On the Road*, he's sure as hell not now. He lives in this little house with his mom. They drink together; she treats him like he's about nine. When the kooks show up, she's the one who scares them away. If it makes you feel any better, he probably doesn't even remember what happened last night."

"Yeah, but *I* remember," I said. "Plus, we never should have been chasing after him in the *first* place. We found out he was down here because his sister died, for Pete's sake. Of all people, I should have had some respect for that."

We were quiet a while, just sitting in my crappy little room. The window was open, but there was no breeze and the air inside was warmer and more humid than the air on the street. The logical thing to do would be to pack up and take the first bus home. Chalk up the past month or so as a stupid, misguided interlude in my real life.

Then Chuck said, "Forget the movie. I haven't talked to Jack since the middle of the Phillies losing streak and, with the Cards taking the pennant, I've been thinking about going over to see him.

You want to come along?"

"I don't know man. I—"

"We'll play it by ear. If he recognizes you from last night, you apologize; if not—" He grinned. "You're Catholic. You just go to confession and the priest lets you off the hook, right?"

I laughed. "Right," I said.

Chuck knew the guy who owned the Tic Toc, too, so we stopped there on the way to Jack's, and he produced my wallet from behind the bar, minus my fake ID. But Mom's picture was there, no worse for the wear. He apologized for the night before. The guys who roughed us up had been way out of line, he said, even though Duke *was* really obnoxious. I was welcome to come back any time—after I turned twenty-one.

"Jack okay?" Chuck asked.

"Tom had to haul his ass out to the car. But he does that a lot of nights, you know?"

"Yeah," Chuck said. "I know."

Tom was Jack's driver, he told me when we got back to the car. Not officially, or anything like that. It was just that Kerouac didn't drive—which was kind of funny, considering he was the guy who wrote *On the Road*—and Tom somehow ended up being the person who took him pretty much everywhere he wanted to go.

Chuck grinned. "Mamère—that's what Jack calls his mom—she can't stand Tom, she won't let him come anywhere near the house. She's convinced that if it weren't for Tom, Jack would be the good Catholic boy he's supposed to be. Me, she's crazy about. You'll see."

It was true. Her weathered face lit up when she opened the door and saw him. "Chuck," she said, with some kind of accent so it sounded like, "Chook."

He leaned down and gave her a hug, then introduced me.

"Ti-Jean," Mrs. Kerouac called, opening the door wider to let us in. "Ti-Jean! Here is Chuck to see you. And his friend."

"It's okay," Chuck said. "We'll come back another time if he's busy."

"You boys wait." She started toward the little hallway, calling out again. "Ti-Jean."

"It's what she calls Jack," Chuck said quietly. "It's French. Well, French Canadian, for—I don't exactly know what."

Moments later, she returned with Jack in tow, a can of beer in his hand, a cigarette between his fingers—wearing the same flannel shirt and baggy unpressed pants he'd worn the night before. His thick black hair was standing straight up, like he'd been running his fingers through it.

He nodded, when Chuck introduced me. If I looked familiar to him, he didn't mention it.

"Sorry, if we disturbed you, man," Chuck said. "I told Mamère we could come back another time. But she said—"

"Always do what Mamère says," Jack interrupted. "*I* always do what she says. Mamère says, 'You come see Chuck, he waits for you,' I come."

She swatted him on the arm. A weird, flirty little swat, the kind Kathy used to give me when she was pretending to be annoyed with me. She spoke to him in French, and he answered in French.

He invited us further in with a sweep of his hand, ashes from his lit cigarette scattering. "She said, 'Tell the boys, sit.'"

We sat. Chuck and I on the couch; Jack on a worn green armchair. He shook a cigarette from an open pack on the table beside him, lit it with the one he'd by now smoked down to almost nothing. He stubbed the old one out, took a long drag from the new one. A huge ginger cat appeared, purring, and leapt into his arms.

Jack's mom brought a Falstaff for Chuck and me, and two for Jack. I thanked her, calling her "Mrs. Kerouac," but she beamed at me and said, no, no, I should call her "Mamère," and that I looked like Ti-Jean when he was a boy. She'd brought a beer for herself, too, and sat down in a rocking chair, sipping it, watching over us.

"Hey, man, what about those Cards taking the pennant?" Chuck asked.

Jack grinned. His eyes were red-rimmed, his face was puffy, and you could see the broken blood vessels on his face—drinkers' veins, I'd heard them called. But he was totally coherent on the subject of baseball. He drained one of the Falstaffs. Then, settling back in his chair, waving his lit cigarette, spouting statistics, he analyzed the run-up to the World Series and why it had come down like it did.

His voice surprised me. So low, sometimes I had to lean forward a little to hear him. There was a hint of an accent: "wi-ah" he said for "wire." "Far" was "fah." He knew everything—league stats, team stats, each player's stats and personal histories, trades, owners, managers, you name it—and what he knew made its way into his commentary naturally, just as it would in a story. In fact, if you could have heard only the sound and rhythm of what he was saying about the pennant race, you might have thought he was reading out loud from *On the Road.*

"Man, what a season," he concluded. He unscrewed the cap from a bottle of Johnny Walker Red that was tucked between the cushion and the side of his chair, and took a swig.

"What's your call, Chuck? Who's going to take the Series?"

"Cards," Chuck said. "Ford's shoulder's wrecked. Mantle's a gimp. Maris—"

"Maris is not a factor," Jack interrupted. "Not a factor. Paul?"

"Hey, I'm a Sox fan," I said. "But now that they're out of the running, I like the Cards for the Series. I love Bob Gibson."

"Oh, yeah," Jack said.

I let the conversation between Chuck and Jack flow, weighing in now and then, taking in my surroundings. The house was small, crowded with shabby furniture. It was dark inside, the windows covered with heavy drapes—probably to keep people like me and Duke from snooping around. There was a crucifix on the wall above

Jack's chair, with dry palm leaves tucked behind it, left over from Lent—and a weird, modern art kind of painting of what I guessed, based on his red robe, the silver crucifix around his neck, and the wide-brimmed black hat he held in one hand, was a cardinal in the church. The place was spotless. Every wood surface shone in the yellow lamplight, there were starched white doilies on every table—except for the one next to Jack's chair, which was cluttered with books and empty beer cans and held an ashtray overflowing with cigarette butts.

I sensed Mamère watching me, but I couldn't help looking at the framed pictures of Jack arranged on a low table, almost like a shrine—one of which I figured was his high-school graduation picture. In it, his hair was neatly cropped; he wore a V-neck sweater, a shirt and tie under it; he gazed directly into the camera. He was not smiling, but he wasn't exactly serious, either. He looked like he was thinking about something secret that pleased him, something inside himself that was totally his own and that he believed was absolutely invulnerable.

Aside from being dark and stocky, I didn't think I looked much like him. But I saw something of myself in the picture, and what I saw is that I was so young. If I could have looked at my own senior picture, I'm pretty sure I'd have seen Jack's secret satisfaction in my expression, that same certainty. What happened to my mom had stripped me of the illusion of invulnerability—mine or anyone else's. Something had stripped Jack of his belief that nothing in the world could hurt him, too. I wondered what it was.

I knew what Duke would say. "All famous writers get wrecked, man. Too much fame, too much booze, too much pussy." He'd provide a litany of wrecked writers to prove his point—in a tone of voice that gave you the idea he was looking forward to the opportunity to being wrecked himself. Adding, in this case, that no matter how rich and famous and wrecked he got, there was no way he'd end up living with his mother.

If he'd been there, he'd have been taking in Mamère: a dumpy little woman, her hair dyed jet black, wearing a faded housedress and those clunky brown tie-shoes old ladies wear. Her apron with a saint's medal pinned to it and a rosary in the pocket, which she took out from time to time, murmuring the black beads. He'd be itching to get it all in his notebook.

Jack drained the second Falstaff; Mamère brought him two more. His eyelids began to droop, his voice slurred, his hands shook. The arms of his chair had little scorched holes all over them, probably from cigarette sparks. Suddenly, he rose and careened toward the back of the house.

"You boys go now," Mamère whispered, nodding toward the door. "Come back. Watch the game with Ti-Jean tomorrow."

"Is he always like that?" I asked Chuck, driving back to town.

"Pretty much," he said. "It's sad."

"Yeah," I said. "What do you think happened to him?"

"*On the Road* happened," Chuck said. "According to most people, anyway. But I don't know. He gave me this book he wrote about his older brother, Gerard, who died when he was nine and Jack was four—and told me it was the best, most important thing he'd ever written. Man, I could hardly get through it. No kidding, it is seriously weird. There's all this stuff in the book about Gerard talking to birds and animals and blessing people. I think Jack actually believes the kid was a saint.

"He talks about him sometimes. Gerard. How he had these visions, how he suffered. What I think is, Jack was already wrecked when he wrote *On the Road*. Getting famous only made it worse. And ending up stuck here in the middle of nowhere with Mamère didn't help, either. He told me his dad made him promise he'd take care of her when he was dying—though it's hard to tell who's taking care of who, since they're both loaded about ninety percent of the time.

"Listen," he added. "If you don't want to watch the game with him, don't feel bad. He's likely to be the same as he was this evening, maybe worse."

"I want to," I said. "But don't you have class?"

"Cutting," he said. "Thursday, too. I've got this girl set up to take notes for me. If the Series goes into next week, I'll cut then, too. I love college, you know? Nobody to tell me what to do, nobody constantly reminding me that baseball—or *whatever*—is the work of the devil."

The Animals came on the radio. "The House of the Rising Sun."

"Shit," Chuck said. "The devil heard me *say* that." He turned the volume up, loud—and the raw, defiant sound of the song filled the night. "I'm doomed," he said. "Who cares?"

I cracked up. "Join the club," I said. "Who knew it would feel so good?"

EIGHTEEN

WEDNESDAY AFTERNOON, GAME TIME, THE TV was on at Jack's house, tuned to the pre-game program, and Chuck and I sat down in the same places we'd sat in before, Jack with the ginger cat in his lap. He tossed Chuck and me a Falstaff from the six-pack on the table beside him. Mamère brought in a plate of salami sandwiches, set it on the coffee table, then settled in her rocking chair with a beer of her own.

Jack looked better today, more alert. He'd shaved; his black hair was still wet from a shower; his pants and shirt fresh from Mamère's iron. He listened intently to what the sportscasters were saying, sometimes nodding in agreement, sometimes arguing as if they were right there in the room with us—leafing through a beat up spiral notebook full of statistics to prove his points.

We all agreed that Mantle's knees were a major factor—especially the right, which, rumor was, he couldn't control unless it was wrapped because the cartilage had turned to jelly.

"The Cards have got to run on him," Jack said.

Chuck nodded. "Absolutely. They've got to run on Mantle. They've got the speed; he can't go after them."

In the first inning, Brock singled with one out—and went to

third when Groat singled to right. Mantle didn't even make a throw.

"Yes, *yes,*" Jack said.

He got up and did a little dance when Mike Shannon came up in the sixth, with two guys on base, and hit the ball so hard it bounced off the "B" in the Budweiser sign.

Not long after, Al Downing replaced Whitey Ford on the mound. "Man, oh, man," Jack crowed, when Ford loped painfully off the field. "What do you want to bet we just saw Whitey's last pitch?"

"Ever?" Chuck asked.

"Ever!" Jack raised his glass.

When it was over and the Cards had won, he passed the bottle of Johnny Walker to Chuck, who took a swig and passed it to me. The whiskey burned going down, and my eyes watered.

Mamère brought more sandwiches. We drank a few more beers. After a while, I got up the nerve to say I really liked *On the Road*, and Jack ducked his head a little, like a kid will do if you embarrass him. Then he invited me to come and see the bookcase in his room where he kept the translations of *On the Road* and his other books. French, Spanish, German, Italian. Some languages I didn't even recognize.

His room was small, neat as a pin. The bookcase, a narrow bed, a dresser, a desk under the window. A bedside table with a radio on it, playing a jazz station, and another one with a small record player on it, a stack of LPs on the shelf beneath.

There was a diagram of a baseball field on one wall, marked with differently shaded circles, which Jack explained stood for different kinds of hits in his fantasy baseball game. Still in a magnanimous mood from the Cards' win, he opened a battered wood box and showed me the hand-drawn index cards, maybe two hundred of them.

On each there was a complicated grid with fielding options and a coded set of possibilities for every aspect of play. You could play it on the board, tossing an eraser at the chart to establish the hit, or you could play with the cards alone. Bigger cards, one for each team in the league, showed a diagram of the field with the first-string players' names at their positions and the other players listed in corner boxes.

"Every team: forty games a season," he said. "Since—what? 1929?"

He showed me the notebooks where he kept the statistics of each game, along with comments on the play. Other notebooks tracked the business end of the league: salaries, injuries, trades, disputes. He told me about the players, their personal lives and histories in the league, and it was as if he was talking about real people. El Negro, Wino Love, Zagg Parker.

He and Chuck offered to play an inning to show me how the game worked.

Jack motioned me to sit down on his desk chair to watch. I was so close to his typewriter that I could have reached out and touched the keys—the very typewriter he'd used to write *On the Road,* for all I knew. I thought of Duke, wondered where he was by now and what he'd think if he could see me here in Jack's bedroom. Barely two days had passed since he left, though it seemed like longer. I didn't think he'd have gotten to San Francisco yet, and I wondered if he'd stopped off to watch the game in a bar someplace, or whether he was still on the bus, listening to it on his transistor radio. Wherever he was, though, I knew he'd be royally pissed off about the Yankees losing.

"Figures he'd be a Yankee fan," Chuck said, when I mentioned this later. "But I bet he'd be even *more* pissed that a guy like me knows Jack Kerouac."

"No doubt," I said.

He laughed. "Guys like that take all the air out of a room, you know?"

"I didn't realize how much energy it took just to be with Duke till he was gone," I said. "Kind of like how the noise in the mill always seemed the worst when I walked out in the morning and it was suddenly so quiet. I've got to say, I don't miss him."

"I hear you," Chuck said. "Still, it's too bad when a friendship doesn't work out. You have some good times, you think you're on the same track, then—"

He shrugged. "You change, they change, or something happens and you realize you didn't really know who they were."

"I never really had a lot of friends," I said. "Partly because I was always with Kathy, but mainly because my brother and I are so close in age we always hung out together. We didn't really need anybody else."

"You miss him?"

"Yeah. I feel bad for ditching out on him, too, for not being able to go to his games. He's good—quarterback. If he plays as well as he did last year, he's likely to get a scholarship. Small school, probably. Still."

I didn't wait for Chuck to ask me about Bobby, but launched into this story about playing baseball in Joey Bucko's back yard when we were kids and how Joey's crabby next-door neighbor, Mrs. Bober, would keep any ball that crossed into her yard

"Then one evening around suppertime, a car lost control, veered off the superhighway that ran behind our subdivision, and crashed through the fence, right into the back of Mrs. Bober's house," I said. "It was wild! Within two minutes, practically everyone in the neighborhood was standing in the Buckos' yard.

"The Bobers were all outside; Mrs. Bober, wailing. A cheer went up, *not* the Bobers, when the car door opened and the driver staggered out and raised his hands to show he was okay. Then there were sirens—an ambulance got there, a fire truck, the police.

"Meanwhile, my brother is cracking us all up, even some of the parents, giving a play-by-play of what was going on, like a sports announcer. So. The fire truck leaves, the ambulance leaves, the policeman heads back to the squad car—at which point, Bobby yells, 'Hey, Mrs. Bober! Since that car landed in your yard, do you get to keep it?'

"Man, it was *dead* quiet. Then everybody started cracking up—except my dad. He grabbed Bobby by the arm, marched him out of the Buckos' yard and over to the Bobers' and made him apologize. Then marched him toward home, hollering for me to follow.

"He grounded Bobby from baseball for the rest of the week. I had to stay in the rest of that evening, for laughing at his rude behavior. Which was totally unfair, because later, when they thought we were asleep, I heard them laughing.

"Dad kept saying it. 'Hey, Mrs. Bober! Since that car landed in your yard, do you get to keep it?' And every time, they'd crack up again. That kind of laughing that hurts your stomach, but you can't stop even if you try."

Chuck smiled. "I like your brother already," he says. "You're lucky to have a family like that, you know?"

"Yeah," I said. "I do."

I changed the subject to Jack's baseball game, asking about some of the more intricate rules. We moved from there to Chuck telling me about how cool it was to be in St. Pete when the Cards were in town for spring training, how Ginny's Uncle Bud had taken Lou Burdette and some of his friends deep-sea fishing last year and Burdette sent him a huge team picture that each player signed— which, in spite of his wife's protests, he'd framed and hung in the living room.

Jack was cranky and agitated when we got to his house to watch game two the next day. His mood darkened with a Yankee win and still hadn't lifted when we came back Saturday for game three. It was tight, both Bouton and Simmons pitching hard. The Yankees scored in the second inning, the Cards evened it up in the fifth and it stayed that way through the eighth. All the while, Jack kept drinking, smoked even more than usual, swore at the television—and squabbled with Mamére when he finished the Johnny Walker, demanding that she bring him his bottle of Thunderbird.

Mantle was one home run away from beating Babe Ruth's World Series record, and when he hammered a pitch from Shultz, Jack left the room without a word, taking the bottle of wine with him. He didn't come back.

"He's a hard guy to be friends with sometimes," Chuck said, driving back to the Y. "Trouble is, you never know which Jack you're going to get. Not to mention, whatever Jack he is at any given moment is likely to do a Dr. Jekyll and Mr. Hyde on you. The thing I really can't stand, though, is when he starts in on the bleeding heart of Jesus and the crown of thorns. That's just too damn weird for me. Or when he gets on one of his tirades about Jewish people or coloreds. *You* know how ugly that one is."

"But he wasn't always like that, was he? *On the Road* isn't like that."

"No," Chuck said. "But it's what he grew up hearing at home—and the truth is, he never really left. He hung out in New York, but most of the time he was *living* with Mamère. He'd take off for California or Morocco or Mexico, which she paid for—working in a factory, for Christ's sake. Listen to her sometime; she's worse than he is. And together—"

Chuck shook his head. "It's pathetic. I know you really love that book," he added. "But I've got to admit, I don't like it that much myself. I mean, what's the point? Bouncing from one place to another, drunk all the time—or high."

"Yeah. There's some truth to that, I said. "I just didn't see it before—"

"Before you actually *met* him," Chuck finished. "Remember that part in *The Catcher in the Rye,* when Holden says that thing about how, when you get knocked out by a book, you wish the author was a friend you could call up on the phone?"

I nodded.

"Be careful what you ask for, huh?"

"Maybe," I said. "On the other hand, I guess it's good to know what's real."

"Like you have the option to go back and *not* know it now," Chuck said. "In any case, I think we could both use a break from the real Jack Kerouac, at least for a little while. I'm glad we're going to Pass-a-Grille to watch the game tomorrow."

NINETEEN

GINNY'S WHOLE FAMILY WAS AT The Palms when we got there: uncles, aunts, cousins, cousins' kids—and her grandparents, who sat on arm chairs brought out from the lobby, shaded by one of the yellow and white striped umbrellas, drinking Bloody Marys. The console television from the lobby had been brought out, too, and set in a corner of the pool deck so you could see it from any angle. Ginny introduced me to everyone, including her Uncle Jimmy, who owned the Crab Shack. An ex-Navy guy, his blond hair was cut in a military buzz, his khaki pants had sharp creases, and his Hawaiian shirt looked like it had just been pressed. He was freckled, like Ginny, but stocky and strong.

He cocked his head and looked at me. "Play?" he asked, when we shook hands.

"Center."

"Any good?"

"Not bad. My brother's better, though."

Jimmy had played football in high school, too, and we talked about the game a little bit.

"You miss it?" he asked.

"Yeah. I'd probably miss it more if I were at home, though. It doesn't feel like fall here, so I don't think about it much. Palm trees just don't bring football to mind, you know?"

Jimmy laughed. "Ginny told me you might be sticking around St. Pete a while," he said. "I need a dishwasher. Morning shift. Early. You want a job, come see me."

"Thank you, sir," I said. "I might just do that."

"Jimmy." He nodded toward Ginny's grandparents. "'Sir' would be my father."

When I'd gotten through all the introductions, Chuck brought me a beer. "So when do you start the job?"

"I don't have a job," I said.

Chuck grinned. "That's you what *you* think."

We helped Ginny haul a bunch of stuff down to the beach, where she planned to take the little kids when the game started.

"Not a baseball fan?" I asked.

"I hate *watching* any kind of game."

"Do you even know who's playing?" Chuck asked.

She shot him a withering glance.

"Okay, who?"

"The Yankees and the Cardinals," she said. "And I'm for the Cardinals, though I'm pretty sure my life won't be wrecked if it doesn't work out that way. Honest to God, it amazes me how you people get so rabid about baseball. Even if I could make myself really, truly care about…*any* team, why would I want to set myself up for that kind of disappointment?"

"The ocean will never let you down," Chuck said.

"Exactly," Ginny said. "Give me any two options of where to be and there's a ninety-nine percent chance the beach is going to be my choice."

"Where's the one percent?" I asked.

She looked surprised by the question. "I don't know," she said. "I've never really thought about that."

Near game time, everyone loaded up their plates with shrimp

and fries and coleslaw that Jimmy had brought over from the Crab Shack. They took their places on an assortment of lounge chairs, lawn chairs, kitchen chairs, and card-table chairs on the pool deck. Some ate in the pool, using the edge like a table. The uncles and cousins who weren't eating watched the game in the pool, floating on rubber rafts.

The uncles and most of the cousins were blond and freckled, like Ginny—like the picture of Ginny's dad I'd seen the last time I visited; even her tiny grandmother had freckles, though they'd faded over time. And while the aunts didn't look like the Benedict family and didn't look alike, either, they all had short, lacquered, beauty-shop hair and wore similar pastel slacks outfits, which made them seem interchangeable.

When Ginny left for the beach with the children at her heels, jockeying for her attention, the conversation turned to how she'd shortened her hours on Shell Key so she could help out at the Crab Shack after her Aunt Mary's surgery and how Jimmy and Mary could not imagine how they'd have managed without her. How you could always count on Ginny to help out. If you needed something, she was right there.

"I wish she'd get out more with people her own age, though," Lo said. "Have some fun."

"Hey," Chuck said. "What am I?"

"Family," Lo said. "You know what I mean."

"Does that Cartwright boy still come around?" one of the aunts asked. "Good Lord, he's been smitten with her since they were children."

"Jerry. He does. He tries to talk her into going to the dances out at the armory, or to a movie. But—"

"He's a good boy," another of the aunts said. "And he comes from a nice family. You watch. She'll open her eyes. For goodness sake, the way she is with the little ones, don't you think she's going to want kids of her own someday?"

Lo rolled her eyes. "Ask her, if you don't mind getting your head bitten off. She'll tell you the same thing she tells me, 'I'm not interested in any of that.'"

The aunts clucked over this for a while, then turned to other family matters, the ebb and flow of their conversation a counterpoint to the hype of the voices calling the game. If they even noticed that things weren't going so well for the Cards in the first five innings, they didn't mention it, except to chide one of the uncles, maybe Dale, for swearing too much.

Spirits lifted when Carl Warwick got a single, followed by another by Flood, and then an error put Groat on first, the bases loaded. Boyer was up. He took the bat from the batboy, swung it a few times—and cracked a grand slam.

The uncles went wild. Chuck, however, didn't say a word, just stood and threw himself into the pool, fully dressed. The rest of the uncles followed, creating a tidal wave that set the women scrambling. I went in, too—thinking about how Dad and Bobby would love this extreme display of happiness and how it turned into a huge melée, everyone splashing and dunking everyone else like a bunch of little kids.

I hadn't talked to my dad since I called him from Nashville, just sent a postcard letting him know I'd made it to Florida and I was okay. Like a postcard would make him stop worrying. I should call home tonight, I thought. It would be easy. "How about that game?" I'd say when Dad or Bobby answered. We'd talk about Boyer's grand slam, I'd tell them about the scene at The Palms. But when my mind got to where I'd go from there, it closed down and I got the same panicky feeling I always got when I thought about calling home, knowing that eventually the conversation would turn to when I was coming home and I'd have to say I wasn't—at least not any time soon.

We got out of the pool, our clothes dripping, the uncles arguing about what the Cards' strategy in game five should be. Chuck and

I went down to the beach to find Ginny, who was helping the kids build an entire sand village, each castle and bridge and tower elaborately decorated with shells they'd collected. One skinny little blond boy, maybe six, kept running back and forth from the town to the ocean to fill his bucket for the ever-draining moat. Clete. This was always his job, Ginny told us. Because he always needed wearing down.

Chuck picked up a bucket and challenged him to a race, which was so totally unfair that it was funny, and pretty soon all the kids abandoned the sand village and pitched in to help their cousin, circling Chuck and hanging on to his knees, finally knocking him over in the sand. It clung to his skin, to his wet clothes and hair.

"You look like a sugar cookie," Ginny said.

At which point, the kids were on him again, trampling the sand village in their pretend-effort to devour him—except for one little girl who burst into tears.

"They ruined it," she wailed, throwing herself into Ginny's arms. "I hate them. I *hate* them. Why did they have to ruin it?"

Ginny let her cry awhile, cradling her, rubbing her back, repeating her name. *Annie, Annie, Annie.* "Remember what we say," she said, when the little girl calmed down.

"But—"

"Remember?" Ginny said again.

Annie nodded, hiccoughing.

"Things go away. We live near the ocean, so we have to get used to that."

Annie nodded again.

"Okay, then." Ginny let her loose, patted her on the bottom and set her moving. "Go get them now!" Annie burst toward the others and threw herself into the fray.

Ginny plopped down on one of the wrinkled beach blankets and signaled me to sit down beside her. "I thought about your question," she said. "The one-percent thing?"

"Yeah?"

"I realized that when I said 'the ocean' I meant right here: this beach. Or Shell Key. Which made the one-percent question easy: the only other place I'd want to be is…some other beach. Which I guess makes me pretty boring."

"Not at all," I said. "I think you're really lucky to know exactly what you want. Chuck does, too. I wish I did."

She gave me a long look, like she was reading me. "Well," she said. "What do you love?"

I thought about it. Baseball. But I wasn't good enough to play professionally, and I didn't want to be a sportswriter, like Chuck did. Or a coach. "I love reading," I said. "But I don't think I love it like you love the ocean. And I don't want to be a teacher, so what good does that do?"

"It would get you through college," she said. "Which is a whole lot better idea than hanging around here, or anywhere, till you get drafted and sent to Vietnam. It's happening already, you know. Two guys from Pass-a-Grille have been drafted in the last six months, for God's sake. A guy I know at school, an ex-Marine, just got back. He says we don't know the half of what's going on over there. They don't *want* us to know. I'm just saying, if you get a college deferment you're not likely to have to go over and find out for sure. Unless you're one of those idiots who think going off to any kind of war automatically makes you a hero."

"I'm not one of those idiots," I said.

I told her about my dad getting a Purple Heart in the war, but refusing to talk about it—and all the books I'd read trying to figure out what it might have been like for him. She'd read *All Quiet on the Western Front* in an English class, and we talked about what war did to people.

Her dad joined the Navy the day after Pearl Harbor, she told me. He'd met her mom the summer before, when she was vacationing with some girlfriends in St. Petersburg.

"My grandparents knew he'd been driving up to see a girl in Atlanta every chance he got," she said. "But they'd never met her. They had no idea it was really serious until he and Mom eloped on his last leave before shipping out. He was the baby of the family. The best-looking of all of them, the best athlete. He was funny and smart—and wild. *Everyone* loved him." She smiled. "So even though my mom was—as you can see, *different* from all the other aunts, not to mention my grandparents, they invited her to come live in Pass-a-Grille while Dad was overseas, and she did. He was on a P.T. boat in the Pacific, which, according to Uncle Jimmy, was the worst duty you could get in the Navy. It changed him. That's all anybody has to say about it."

She scooped up some sugar sand and let it sift through her fingers. She did it again, watching it fall as if watching the sand fall in an hourglass. Then looked directly at me. "Sometimes I think he loved me so much because I was the only one who hadn't known him before the war. He couldn't disappoint me.

"So. Don't get drafted," she concluded brusquely, before I had a chance to speak. "And I repeat: If you go to college, that's not likely to happen."

"You've got a point," I said.

"Yes," she said. "I do. So take that job Jimmy offered you and start saving up for it."

TWENTY

So there I was the next morning, washing dishes at the Crab Shack. Jimmy had given me explicit directions: Soak the dishes first, plunge them into scalding water, let them air dry. He handed me a pair of yellow rubber gloves so I wouldn't burn my hands, a white apron to keep my clothes clean, and a bandana to tie, Indian-style, around my head to keep the sweat under control. Any time there was a lull in the action, he checked on me to make sure the dishes were as sparkling clean as he expected them to be—nodding his satisfaction.

Meanwhile, Ginny zoomed up and down the counter, taking orders, pouring coffee, asking about wives and kids and grandkids, commiserating about the snowbirds who were already starting to clog traffic up and down the beach highway, delivering the heaping portions of eggs and bacon and oatmeal and pancakes, then bringing the dirty dishes back into the kitchen and setting them on the drain board to be washed. Now and then stopping long enough to ask if I was doing okay.

I was. I liked being busy and, even though an earnest half-wit could have done the job the way Jimmy wanted it done, I still felt good about doing something right. The dishes kept coming; I kept washing them. Standing there in the cloud of steam, I saw Mom in my mind's eye, ironing, steam puffing up from the iron, and I remembered how she always said she didn't mind ironing because you could see the progress you were making—plus, you could listen to the radio and daydream, which made time pass quicker than you'd think. For once, it didn't make me sad to think about her—maybe because washing dishes felt exactly the same way.

It was a good day all around. Chuck and I met at Jack's to watch the fifth game. He was in a great mood, convinced that Boyer's grand slam had put the Cards on a roll. They'd win again today; Wednesday, back in St. Louis, it would be all over. Best of all, when the game actually started it was clear that, for the first time in the Series, the real Bob Gibson was back in the game. The guy was a strikeout machine, his face like a robot. The Yankees didn't know what to do with him.

Jack drank steadily throughout the game, and the win made him manic with happiness. He danced Mamère around the little house until she was beet red and breathless, begging him to let her go before she had—as she said—an attack of the heart. He wouldn't let Chuck and me leave, but kept us pinned to our seats, telling us about his dad taking him to Boston Red Sox games when he was a kid; jumping from there to Yankee Stadium and New York itself—hanging out there with his friend, Neal, the real Dean Moriarity.

He was still ramped up when Chuck and I came back for game six, still sure it would wind up the Series for the Cards, and already drinking toward the celebratory moment. It was weird, as if the liquor inside him knew when the Yankees pulled away in the seventh inning, because, suddenly, it turned him ugly. He was in a rage by the time Pepitone finished it off with a grand-slam homer in the ninth: rude to Mamère, argumentative if anybody said anything to disagree with him, and belligerent when Chuck tried to settle him down.

"Okay, I'm done," Chuck said, when we left. "I've seen him like this before. He's so far gone it won't matter who wins the last game. Even if he's not passed out somewhere by then, he'll be too hungover to have any idea what's going on. Once he gets going on these binges, nothing can stop him. Sometimes it's weeks before he gets back to normal." He laughed, but not like he thought anything was funny. "Like Jack's 'normal' is a great way to be."

There was a TV at the Crab Shack. We'd watch it there, we decided. We gathered with Jimmy and a bunch of the regulars, a few tourists who just happened in and stayed. Ginny skipped class to stick around and help wait tables.

It was a Cards crowd. Jimmy had put a sign on the door that said: "Yankee fans, enter at your own risk." A joke—well, sort of— but it kept them away. Jimmy was wearing a Cards tee-shirt; most of the old guys were wearing St. Louis baseball caps set back on their heads, like old guys do.

This was it: Either the Yankees or the Cards were going to win the Series today—and it was tense. Gibson was clearly tired, but the Cards stayed on top. It was 6-0 till the sixth, when Mantle smashed a three-run homer. The Cards scored again in the seventh, but in the bottom of the ninth the Yankees scored twice—pulling them to within two runs, with one out still to go.

Should they leave Gibson in? Take him out?

They left him in.

The next batter popped to the Cards' shortstop, who made the catch—and it was over.

The whole Crab Shack went nuts. All of us yelling and throwing our arms around each other and pounding on whatever or whoever happened to be near. It must have been contagious because even Ginny was ecstatic, dancing in and out of everyone's embrace.

The place felt like home to me after that day. Every morning I got up at five and walked through the quiet streets to the pier, which was already lined with fishermen who stood, their lines out, drinking coffee they poured into the plastic lids of their Thermoses. I got there about 5:30, and Jimmy greeted me, already on his second or third cup of coffee. We set up for the day, talking about this and that.

The mornings went quickly once Ginny arrived and tied on her apron. I was my own little assembly line, moving the dishes from one side of the sink to the other, all the while daydreaming, half-hearing the music on Jimmy's little radio. Most days Ginny and I ate lunch together, sitting out on the pier, talking, watching the water. She refused to eat meat or, God forbid, any of her beloved sea creatures, and I teased her about that. She needed a good cheeseburger, I'd say, and she'd tell me it was none of my goddamn business what she ate. Nothing she did was any of my business, for that matter. She was serious.

I didn't mind. I liked how she treated me like she was my big sister: bossy, with a kind of eye-rolling affection. I liked how I could talk to her about anything. I told her the things about when Mom was sick that I most hated remembering. The way her head looked, shaved for surgery, and how scared she'd been. How, in the beginning, she kept saying, "But I'm a good person. I'm a good person," as if the brain tumor were God's punishment for something she'd done. How, when the headaches came back near the end, she didn't know me. She thought I was her brother, who'd been killed in a car accident when he was twenty.

One day I was telling her for about the tenth time how bad I felt about ditching Kathy after how great she'd been while Mom was sick and after she died. "She did everything for me," I said. "My laundry, for Christ's sake; *all* of our laundry. And came over most nights and made dinner for us. Then did the dishes."

Always before Ginny had listened, nodding her head as if in sympathy with me. Now, sounding half-mad, she said, "You didn't *need* a personal maid, Paul. What you *needed* was someone who understood how you felt."

Instinctively, I defended Kathy. "She tried. She really did. She about drove me crazy, constantly asking me how I felt."

"How *do* you feel?" Ginny asked.

It sounded different when she asked, like she was genuinely curious.

"Well," I said. "Remember that earthquake in Alaska in March? Part of Anchorage sliding into the ocean, part of Kodiak wiped out by a tidal wave, stuff blowing up and burning? That was how I felt," I said.

"And you told that to Kathy?"

"I did. But she took it the wrong way, like nothing she'd done for me had mattered. I knew there was no point trying to explain. And I didn't dare apologize because I knew if I apologized she'd forgive me and try harder to make me feel better, when what I really wanted was for her, for *everybody*, to just leave me alone."

"If she *really* knew you, she'd have known that's what you wanted," Ginny said.

"Maybe," I said. "Still, it's no excuse. The truth is, I was awful to her from the time I started working at the mill."

"Because she started pushing you to get married."

"Well, yeah. But I'm the one who let her *act* like my wife. Naturally, she'd assume—"

"Paul," Ginny said. "Almost *all* girls want to get married the first second they possibly can. They're stupid that way. Haven't you figured that out yet? And boys are stupid about sex. You're lucky she didn't get pregnant and trap you into it. Some girls do that, you know."

I opened my mouth to say that Kathy wouldn't have done that to me, but shut it because, suddenly, I wasn't so sure.

"My idiot cousins," she went on, flushed with aggravation. "Trish and Janet. They couldn't wait to get out of Pass-a-Grille and head for the big city—and what are they doing there? Looking for husbands. All they talk about when they come home to visit is getting married and settling down. The house in suburbia, a bunch of kids to take care of, watching TV, grilling out on the weekends… just not *here*. I mean, really, what's the point?

"You get one life," she said. "One. Life. I want mine to be larger than that."

A silence fell between us, the kind that happens after bells ringing. I'd never heard anyone, male or female, say anything like that. I had no idea how to respond to it.

"Sorry," Ginny said, after a while. "I get a little crazy about things like that. Anyway. Kathy. She sounds like a good, well-meaning person—and you're right, just leaving was a really shitty way to break up with her. On the other hand, you had to get the hell out of there to save your life. Right?

"And okay—" She looked like she'd just swallowed a dose of awful-tasting medicine. "As much as I hate to admit this, if Duke was the one who talked you into leaving to come down here, I guess he can't be all bad."

This cracked me up.

But it was another thing I like about Ginny: she told the truth, no matter what.

I felt good when I was with her: things fell into place. In fact, talking to her felt so good that it took me a while to realize that she hardly ever talked about herself—and when she did it was about the work she was doing on Shell Key and the future she planned.

She'd get a Ph.D. in marine biology, teach at the university, do research, and write books about the ocean, books that would make people love it as much as she did. She'd buy a little house of her own on Pass-a-Grille and live in it her whole life—with nobody to answer to but herself.

Personal things? Forget it.

She'd always been like that, Chuck said. Private. She went on dates in high school, but never had a boyfriend. She never had a best girlfriend, either. She made it a point to like everybody just the same.

He grinned. "I like to think that if all of us were drowning and there was only one life jacket, I'd be the one she'd throw it to. But I wouldn't bet on it."

I didn't pry. I admired her. She was so small and fierce, barreling toward her dreams. Why would I want to mess with that?

TWENTY-ONE

THE DAYS CAME AND WENT. Afternoons, when Ginny left for class, I might borrow the rod and reel Jimmy kept at the restaurant and fish for a while with some of the old guys, or walk over to the library and read. Sometimes I took the bus to Haslam's and bought a used book or two. It was still so much like summer that I might not have noticed time passing at all, except for the bats and vampires and kid-sized mannequins dressed in ghost and witch and skeleton costumes decorating the dimestore window. At home, the trees would start to change color; football nights would be cool enough to need a jacket. Pretty soon, kids would be jumping in piles of leaves, carving pumpkins.

A year ago, I was helping build the senior class's *Beowulf*-themed homecoming float in Kathy's backyard. We worked all day one Saturday and Sunday, the number of volunteers growing so that by the middle of the next week, thirty or forty people were there every night to help.

Kathy strung extension cords out of her bedroom window and put her record player on a card table under a big maple tree, setting stacks of 45s on the spindle to play while we worked. The Beach Boys, Jan & Dean, the usual girl groups—and, of course, multiple plays of "My Boyfriend's Back," at which point all the girls would stop stuffing crepe paper and sing at the top of their lungs.

Sometimes I'd just stand back and watch Kathy for a while. Dressed in a pair of wool Bermuda shorts and knee socks and a school sweatshirt or one of my old football jerseys, she was either laughing and stuffing green crepe paper in rhythm to whatever song was on the record player, or in her take-charge mode, checking her clipboard, assigning people to various tasks. If she caught me idle, she'd grab my arm and march me over to do whatever she wanted me to do, which was funny rather than annoying because I got a kick out of her being so obsessed. And she looked so pretty, her cheeks as pink as the last of Mom's roses in the brisk fall air. When she got me where she wanted me to be, I stood stock-still and refused to work until she kissed me.

"Paul," she'd say.

But every time she kissed me, for real, and I'd go back to stuffing crepe paper or use my pocket knife to cut out the big letters of the slogan, "Dragon Down the Archers" from the heavy cardboard where she had traced them—all the while thinking about being alone with her, later, when everyone had gone.

Her birthday had fallen the night before the homecoming game. After we'd made the finishing touches on the float, we sang "Happy Birthday" and ate the cake and ice cream her mom brought out. Later, at our place by the river, I gave her the gold circle pin with a pearl set into it that I'd seen her admire in a jewelry shop window. It made me happy, watching her face light up when she opened the box. We kissed a while, then scrambled into the backseat the way we always did then, unbuttoning, unzipping, still kissing as we went. It hurt sometimes, our arms and legs like tentacles, our bodies ramming into each other as if to break each other open and rush into each other's very being. Then the explosion that left us weak, breathing as if we'd been running instead of making love.

The next night, we won the game and Kathy reigned as

homecoming queen at the dance afterward. A few weeks later, we were on our way to New York. Not long after we got back, I found out my mom was dying.

After the world shifted, Kathy and I had never again made love the way we'd made love the night of her birthday. In the months my mom was sick and after she had died, what I wanted was the feel of Kathy's body, warm against mine. I wanted to hold her. We'd lie in the backseat of the car, wrapped in each other's arms, breathing as if we were one person. I'd drift off to that place you go right before sleep sometimes, half there with Kathy, half in the dreamlike succession of images playing in my head, and when she began to give me light kisses on my neck, pressing the whole length of her body against mine, it felt real and not real, something that took me away from the sorrow and confusion of my real life for a little while.

What if the universe could reset and offer up a different future, one without Mom dying in it? Maybe that future would include finding *On the Road* on our trip to New York, maybe it wouldn't. If it did, maybe I'd break up with Kathy on account of it. Maybe we'd argue, make up and, eventually, get married and live happily ever after. Who knew?

But I couldn't go back—and with Mom gone I didn't want to go back, no matter how many options there might be now that getting married to Kathy was no longer in the picture. I liked the life I was living, washed up at the ocean's edge. I liked having Chuck and Ginny in it.

I liked seeing movies together, playing volleyball on the beach, talking and laughing and arguing for hours over coffee in some crummy little diner. They studied at the library on campus most weeknights until it was time for Chuck to clock in at the Y, and sometimes they talked me into going with them, and I'd just sit and read while they worked.

I read *Cat's Cradle*, which Chuck lent me—then *Mother Night* and *Player Piano* and *The Sirens of Titan*, feeling proud of the fact that Kurt Vonnegut had grown up in Indiana. I read *Invisible Man* and *Black Like Me* and *Johnny Got His Gun*—each one its own mind-bending little universe. I read *One Flew Over the Cuckoo's Nest,* which seriously messed with my head.

It was about this petty criminal who claimed he was crazy so he could get committed to a mental hospital instead of serving jail time, but it turned out that the ward he was assigned to was controlled by this Nazi-like nurse, Miss Ratched. The patients were all too scared to stand up to her, but this guy, McMurphy, decided to bring her down. The problem was, he didn't realize till too late that a jail sentence is finite, but if you get sent to a mental hospital, the doctors decide when you'll be released—which might be never. And the doctors were afraid of Nurse Ratched, too. So he was stuck there, totally at her mercy.

What *is* crazy, I wondered—and who got to decide? What if the person with the authority was mean and vindictive and maybe a little crazy herself? When was it okay—maybe even wrong *not*—to break the rules? If you convinced people to break the rules with you, what was your responsibility toward them?

Was it *ever* okay to alter someone's brain?

I'd heard of shock treatments, but never quite understood what they were until I read that book. I thought lobotomies were a joke, something made up for horror movies. I had no idea that real people had them—whether they wanted them or not. It scared the shit out of me to think about what that would be like.

On the other hand, what if it worked? What if I could lie down on a table, get hit with a couple of bolts of electricity or maybe have a little operation guaranteed to make all the memories of Mom sick and dying go away? Forever.

Wouldn't I be crazy *not* to do that?

One overcast day, I was rereading Hemingway's stories in the public library and glanced up to see that the sky framed by the tall windows had grown dark, almost purple. The palm trees were swaying like dancers in the wind. Then there was a crack and the rain started, lashing the windows, pounding the roof.

The florescent lights in the library seemed suddenly brighter; they took on a strange cast that made my reflection appear in the window across from where I sat. I could also see the reflections of one, then another and another of the down-and-out men as they came into the library through the main door, soaking wet, and quietly took seats around me. Like ghosts.

Hemingway had written those stories in a café in Paris, homesick for Michigan, for the clear vision of the world he had when he was a boy there. I got to the last story, "Indian Camp," and I knew the Indian man in the top bunk was going to slit his throat because he couldn't stand the sound of his wife suffering in childbirth. I knew the last line by heart, but reading it that day totally unhinged me.

Not because the boy's innocence had shocked me into realizing I'd die myself one day. I'd known that, really known it, since I was seven, lying in bed at dusk on a summer evening and the knowledge floated in, as if through the open window. *Someday you will not be.* My heart raced, my blood felt cold inside me. I had to make myself lie still instead of jumping up and running—I didn't even know where, just running away from what I knew. Since then, it would sometimes come upon me just like that, always when I least expected it.

Now, because of Mom, I knew what death looked like—which made it worse. But what hit me that afternoon was what it must have been like for my dad to watch Bobby and me watch Mom die, wanting to protect us because that's what parents did, but helpless in the face of what was happening to us all. I'd sent that one postcard; I still hadn't gotten up the nerve to call him. For all he knew, I could be dead, like Mom—or in some kind of terrible trouble.

Maybe I was like Schrodinger's Cat in his mind, neither dead nor alive until somebody opened the box—and that somebody had to be me. But I didn't want to open it because when I did my other life would flood into it. The one in which Mom was even more dead than she was in the life I was living now.

Dead is dead. I knew that, too. But it didn't feel that way.

I tucked the Hemingway book into my knapsack, got up, elbowed my way through more men coming inside to escape the weather, and burst through the big front doors. I had no idea where I was going; I just knew I didn't want to stay there, among all the wrecked men, whose families probably didn't know where they were, either. Maybe, by now, they didn't even care.

The hard, cold rain shocked me after the damp warmth of the reading room. It felt like a thousand needles on my face, but it was a good hurt, real, and I stood there on the steps of the library I don't know how long, my head raised, taking some weird comfort in knowing the pain was manageable. I could make it stop.

It was so *stupid*, thinking about what might have happened, thinking about alternate lives—real or imagined. I had one life, that's all—and Mom dying, dad loving me and worrying about me and caring about what happened to me would always be in it. I walked to the banyan tree and sat in the little cave of it until I started breathing like a normal person again. I went back to the Y and changed into dry clothes before I met Chuck and Ginny for dinner at Wolfie's.

But Ginny took one look at me and asked, "Paul, what's wrong?"

"Nothing," I said. "I'm fine."

She didn't press me, but she knew I was lying.

TWENTY-TWO

A FEW DAYS LATER, SHE invited me to go out to Shell Key with her. We headed for Pass-a-Grille in her green VW Bug after the lunch rush at the Crab Shack—top down, radio blaring. News to me: Ginny had a boat, too, which she kept at Merry Harbor, a sweet little Chris-Craft her dad owned when he was in high school and her uncles had refurbished for her sixteenth birthday. The honey-colored wood was waxed and gleaming, the chrome fittings shone.

"Slipper Shell" was written in script on the side.

"It's named for sailing slipper shells with my dad," she explained, and took the key to the boat from the battered army duffel retrieved from her locker in the marina. It was attached to a yellow float, along with a shell that had a hole drilled through it, which she held so that I could see the dried membrane that half-covered the scooped out part.

"See? It's like a little bedroom slipper," she said. "But it's like a little boat, too. If you get a perfectly shaped, perfectly balanced one—like this one—you can float it in calm water. It's my absolute first memory: my dad looking for just the right one, then showing me how to float it in a tidal pool. I was three, maybe four years old. We spent hours doing that. I spent hours doing it by myself after he died."

She laughed, which surprised me.

"Sweet little shells," she said. "But get how they mate: they stack up on each other, maybe eight high—males on top so their sex organs can protrude down into the females beneath. Weird enough, right? But here's what I love. When the females die, the males above them turn to females—so there's always a female on the bottom to make babies."

She looked at me, her face radiant with delight. But I was embarrassed, and not for the first time, by the matter-of-factness about which she talked of such things. I was embarrassed about *being* embarrassed. It's just biology, I told myself. What's the big deal?

She hopped down into the boat and gestured for me to follow. She lifted one of the red leather seats and took out two life jackets, putting one on herself and handing me the other. When I'd secured mine to her satisfaction, she donned a battered sailor hat, brim down, started the engine, and off we went, leaving Pass-a-Grille behind us.

It was a slow wake zone, and I sat back, letting the sun wash over me, enjoying the cool sea breeze. Ginny pointed out Tierra Verde to the west—once sacred to the Indians, who used it as ceremonial and burial grounds until the Spanish explorers tried to claim it. Ponce de León was mortally wounded on Tierra Verde, she said.

Ponce de León. All I could remember of him was a picture in my freshman World History book—a guy in old-fashioned clothes, wearing a feathered hat—and something about the Fountain of Youth. But he had been a real person who'd been in this place, where I was now. Pirates and buccaneers had been here, too.

"People still look for the treasure he supposedly buried somewhere on the island," Ginny said. "We used to do it when we were kids. We never found any—but more than once we scared ourselves half to death, convinced that we'd seen ghosts. Especially when we were there at night. My uncle Mike is an amateur astronomer and Shell Key is a great place for stargazing, because it's so dark. So we'd come over—the whole family—and camp out and look at the stars. We can do that sometime, if you want."

"That would be cool," I said. "Where I grew up, you can barely see anything in the sky because of all the crap from the factories."

"It's terrible what we do to the earth," Ginny said. "That stupid bridge they made from the mainland to the St. Pete beaches— as soon as it was possible to drive over there, developers started getting dredge and fill permits. All those new hotels and restaurants everyone is so proud of—if you know what you're looking for, you can actually *see* how altering the shoreline to build them is affecting the balance of things. The erosion on the beaches, the nesting habits of shorebirds."

Out to the east, in open water, porpoises arced up and disappeared beneath the waves.

"They *talk* to each other," Ginny said, her blue eyes suddenly brimming with tears. "Porpoises. They use certain sounds to alert each other to danger, to keep track of each other. That just kills me, you know? That supposedly dumb mammals would take care of each other like that, while we—"

She shook her head and fell silent, navigating the boat away from Tierra Verde toward Shell Key. As we approached, what had been just a green haze in the distance became a beach, sea grasses, palm trees, and pines. Ginny was always talking about doing research for her classes here, so I figured there'd be a laboratory with biologists bent over microscopes. But as far as I could tell, the island looked a lot like it must have looked to Ponce de León more than four hundred years ago.

"It's a living lab," she explained. "One of the last unspoiled barrier islands in the area. Some of it's protected, a reserve—but a big part of it is a public beach with some of the best shelling on the Gulf Coast. There are signs posted around the island to remind people why it's so important to keep it unspoiled. But they still camp too close to the nesting areas. They bring their dogs and let them roam free. Don't even get me started on the trash they leave behind.

"That's what we need to do today, in fact. Pick up trash. Then check the nests and make sure they're safe, rope off any new ones we find."

She cut the engine, dropped the anchor, and we climbed out of the boat and waded to the shore, where she took off at her usual pace, her duffel bag slung over her shoulder. I had to laugh, thinking of what Chuck would say if he could see me hurrying to catch up with her.

We walked the public beach, stopping along the way so Ginny could check off the nesting areas on her clipboard. She told me the names of the birds as we went, both their common and scientific names. Now and then, she stopped, picked up a shell, and told me the name of it, too.

"My dad used to do this with me," she said. "He carried me in his arms even before I could walk, telling me the names of things. When I got older, we'd go out at low tide and throw shells and sand dollars back into the water just in case they might still be alive.

We walked quietly awhile, Ginny darting up into the grasses to check the nests. When she found a new one, I helped her stake it off—and when I picked up the duffel afterwards, she let me carry it. Heading back toward the boat, we took off our shoes and waded along the shore. The air had cooled; the sun was setting earlier now, and soon it would begin its descent into the water.

"They never found his body," Ginny said, still walking. "That made it harder for my family—especially my mom and my grandma. But I was only seven when it happened, and I couldn't figure out why, if he couldn't be here, they wouldn't want him to be in the ocean. I knew they buried dead people. I knew he wouldn't want that. It made me feel better, knowing that's where he was. I'd imagine him swimming with all the beautiful fish, sleeping in the ocean caves he used to show me pictures of. He seemed real as anything."

"Sometimes I think of my mom like that," I said. "But in the kitchen, in the yard."

She stopped and looked at me. "Is that why you don't go home?" she asked. "Because if you're there, you can't pretend everything's okay?"

Now I was the one who kept walking. "I don't know. Maybe."

I changed the subject to the presidential election, just a week away. All the polls had LBJ winning, but the outside chance that Goldwater might just surprise everyone and edge him out was enough to keep people talking about it.

"He's completely insane," Ginny said. "Him and his goddamn nuclear bombs. You read *Hiroshima*. My God. Some people were unrecognizable afterwards; their *faces* melted. They had horrible medical problems from breathing in the poison. But did you know that the bombs also killed everything in nature within a huge radius of where they exploded? Plants, animals, fish, birds. Every. Single. Thing.

"Because *most* people don't know that. They also don't know that a lot of the pesticides we use are doing the same thing right now, just not that dramatically—and if we keep it up, we'll destroy the whole planet. DDT, for example—when we were kids, a truck would come around and spray that stuff practically every night in the summer to kill the mosquitoes. We thought it was so cool; we'd all run after it."

"Yeah," I said. "We did that."

"Everybody our age did," Ginny said. "The thing is, DDT is like a little mushroom cloud in its own right. Sure, it kills the mosquitoes, but it also kills everything else that gets in its way. When they sprayed the salt marshes for mosquitoes a few years ago, it killed almost all the fiddler crabs that fed there. The runoff that got into the ocean killed oysters and clams—and the ones that didn't die showed traces of the poison. Which means people who ate them also ingested it. Who knows what might happen to them?

"And crop dusting? The pesticides from that get into whatever you eat in Indiana—" She waved her hands, as if to capture an example. "Corn," she said. "It's pathetic the way we take the earth for granted. It's here. We think it'll always be here. But it won't be, if we don't start paying attention—at least not so anything but cockroaches can actually live on it. You have to make people love the earth. Or at least—

"Sorry," she said. "I'm doing it again."

But I liked that about her, how she was so passionate about what she loved—and I said so, which made her blush.

"And you're right about Goldwater," I added. "My dad pegged him from the start. A rich guy who thinks he can do whatever he damn well pleases. Including bomb the shit of out of whoever disagrees with him."

"What's he like, Paul?" she asked. "Your dad? You've told me a lot about your mom, but you don't say much about him at all."

I thought a moment. "Dad's a good guy. He was nuts about my mom. Seriously. It was like they were still in high school. He's smart. Funny. You'd get a kick out of him."

I told her about our neighborhood, one of those subdivisions that sprung up after the war: six blocks of boxy little houses that looked so much alike, my dad liked to joke that if you had a little too much to drink one night you might end up in your neighbor's bedroom.

The developer had named it Happy Homes.

"That is guaranteed," Dad said, pen poised to sign the mortgage contract. "The happy part. Right?"

The salesman gets this look on his face, like, is this guy *crazy?* Then he pastes a smile on his face and says, "'My goodness. Who wouldn't be happy in a lovely new home like this?'"

Ginny laughed. "How often do you talk to him?"

I shrugged.

She looked at me, I looked away.

"You *don't* talk to him?" she asked. "Paul, does your dad even know where you are?"

"I sent him a postcard when I got here. He knows I'm fine."

"Fine?" she said. "I'm sure your dad does *not* think you're fine. Jesus, Paul. You love him. He's been through hell, losing your mom. And you refuse to talk to him?"

"I'm not *refusing* to talk to him," I said, and kept walking.

"Okay," Ginny said. "Let me get this straight. You sent him one crappy postcard nearly two months ago. You haven't called him; he has no idea how to get in touch with you. What would your name for that be?"

"I know I need to call him, okay? I'm just not ready."

She grabbed my arm, made me stop and look at her. "Don't you think it's time to stop acting like a guilty little kid who ran away from home? Listen, you need to call your father—*now*—and tell him you're not, I don't know, dead or robbing grocery stores to be able to eat. I mean it."

"Okay, okay," I said. "I'll call him."

"Tonight," she said.

"Yeah. Okay. I'll call him tonight."

We'd been invited for dinner at Jimmy's and, when we got there, the house was full of the good smell of spaghetti sauce. Ginny's Aunt Mary stopped stirring and stepped forward, a potholder in each hand, her cheeks flushed, to give us each a hug.

"Jimmy tells me you're doing a wonderful job at the restaurant," she told me. "A high compliment from Mr. Perfection himself."

"Hey," Jimmy said, coming into the kitchen. "I heard that."

Mary put one hand to her heart. "Oh, dear. I guess you didn't know we all thought that about you. I'm so sorry."

"Ha." He put his arm around her, gave her a quick kiss. "You know, she had that damn surgery just to get out of working with me for a while," he says. "Too much pressure. She can't hack it."

Mary swatted him with a potholder and pushed him away. "Sit" she said. "Let Ginny and me get dinner on the table."

It was nice feeling like part of a family, Mary and Jimmy talking about their days, asking Ginny and me about our afternoon on Shell Key. I should invite Dad and Bobby to come down to Pass-a-Grille for Thanksgiving, Mary said. Lo would be glad to make a place for them at The Palms.

"Perfect," Ginny said. "Paul's calling his dad tonight. He can ask him then. You are calling him, right?"

I nodded.

"Well?" she asked.

Mary looked at me, then at Ginny. "For heaven's sake, don't be so darn bossy," she said.

"Me? Bossy?" Ginny asked.

We all laughed.

Ginny lent me her Bug to drive back to St. Pete; she'd hitch a ride to the Crab Shack with Jimmy in the morning. I could have called him from the pay phone at the Y, but I didn't know how the call would go and if I got into an argument with dad or just plain broke down, I didn't want Chuck, or anyone else, to be there. So I kept driving. Past Wolfie's, past the library and Mirror Lake, past Haslam's, the Tic Toc. I drove down to the darkened pier, then turned and took Central Avenue back over the bridge to the beach at Treasure Island, where I parked and walked out onto the sand.

It was deserted. The concession shacks and tacky souvenir shops were closed, the row of lifeguard chairs along the shoreline, empty. I climbed up into one of them and sat, I don't know how long, just looking out. Both sky and water were black, indivisible, the few bits of light I saw might have been the lights of ships moving toward some destination; they could have been stars.

Call, I told myself. Get it over with. Go on from there.

I climbed down, headed toward the phone booth I'd seen near the parking lot. It was late by then, nearly eleven. I remembered how Mom and Dad always stayed up to watch at least part of Johnny Carson on *The Tonight Show*, and I stood for a long moment in the dark booth, imagining the two of them on the couch in the living room, the low rise and fall of their voices mingling with the sound of the television I used to hear, drifting off to sleep.

I put some coins in, took a deep breath, dialed.

"Paul?" Dad said, before I spoke. "Is that you?"

"Yeah," I said. "I'm sorry I haven't called before."

It was quiet for what seemed like an hour.

"Dad—?"

"I'm here," he said, his voice breaking. "It's just—I've been so worried about you, son. It's so good to hear your voice."

"I'm sorry," I said again. "Listen, I'm still in Florida. St. Petersburg. I've got a job. I'm staying at the Y."

"The boy you worked with at the mill—"

"Duke. He took off for California a while back. I wanted to stay in one place for a while. I like it here, Dad. It's so different from home. It's really beautiful, and the ocean—"

"Your mom always wanted to go back to Florida," he said. "I wish—"

"I know. Me, too. I miss her, too."

Then we were both crying—silently, the way we did when she died. Me hunched over in the phone booth, my face hidden to anyone who might be passing by.

"How's Bobby," I asked, when I collected myself.

"He's had a tough time. But—" Dad's voice brightened here. "He's having a great season. There was a piece about him in the sports section last week. It was real good for him. And I think, playing the way he's been, he's getting some of that anger out of his system. He got his license, finally. He's tooling around in your mom's car. That's good, too. "

"Yeah," I said. "He always wanted his license, that's for sure. It's cool that he's doing so well. Tell him I said it's cool, okay?"

"I'll do that," he said.

He asked me about my job, and I told him all about the Crab Shack.

"It's good for now," I said. "You know, until I figure out what I really want to do."

"Think you'll settle there?" Dad asked. "In St. Pete?"

"I don't know. Maybe. I've made some good friends. Plus, there's a college here, and I'm thinking—"

"Your mom had her heart set on college for you boys," he said. "I don't know what I was thinking when I was so quick to let you take the job at the mill—"

"It's okay, Dad. I didn't have the heart for it then. I wasn't ready."

Then he said, "Kathy came by again the other day. She asked if I thought she should wait for you to come back, and I told her no, she had her own life to live. We—talked."

"Oh, shit," I said. "I'm really sorry you had to do that."

"Language," he said, with a smile in his voice. "Listen, son. It was partly my fault, what happened. I should have been paying more attention. We'll call it even, okay?"

"I guess. Okay—and I'll write her a letter. I think I can do that now."

"That would be a good thing," he said.

We talked about the Series, commiserated about the White Sox ending up just one game out in the pennant race. Second place, again.

"Next year," we said, like always.

I promised I'd call every week from now on, and we said goodbye. I sat awhile on the bench in the phone booth, the receiver still in my hand—the sound of Dad's voice echoing in my ears, the image of him alone in the living room in my mind's eye—missing him and Bobby. Missing myself, with them.

TWENTY-THREE

I DROVE AIMLESSLY FOR A while, then I got it in my head that touching base with Jack would somehow be like touching base with who I was before I took off with Duke to find him—and maybe give me some idea of what to do next.

I hadn't seen him since the last Series game we watched together, a few weeks before—and, even if I'd had the nerve to knock on the door and invite myself in for a visit, it was too late for that. My plan was to drive over to his house, sit outside, and just think for a while before going back to the Y. But when I parked and switched the engine off, the night was filled with the most beautiful music I'd ever heard, like a thousand angels singing. It was coming from Jack's open windows and, before I knew it, I was out of the car, darting across the street, ducking into the unkempt shrubbery in his yard, where I crouched beneath his bedroom window, my heart pounding in my ears.

When I calmed down, I heard the sound of typewriter keys tapping beneath the voices, the ding of the bell at the end of a line, the return of the carriage. Sometimes the typing was fast, sometimes slow; sometimes in terse combinations that sounded like Morse code, sometimes almost in rhythm with the music.

Cigarette smoke drifted from the open window, mingling with the sharp scent of the cypress tree that towered over the little house.

I thought of that night in Greenwich Village, barely a year ago, turning my back on Kathy and walking into what I saw now was the beginning of my real life. I saw the little bookshop. I saw myself picking up *On the Road*. I saw the words themselves, which sent me on the journey that had brought me to this hiding place beneath Jack Kerouac's window listening to him write.

I saw Duke that summer night at the mill, standing before the Eddies, shouting up at the stars. If he were with me, he'd try to catch a glimpse of Jack through the open window—then run like hell if he saw us.

I was glad to be alone. I wanted to leave Jack at peace with his words. It was enough just to listen to the music that the voices and his typewriter made together and wonder about the story coming to life beneath his fingers. My eyes grew heavy and, leaning against the house, I dozed off again and again, awakened each time when my head dropped to my chest.

Then, suddenly, the yowling of a catfight jolted me fully awake. I could see them in the light of the moon: two huge cats going at each other like dervishes. Adrenaline coursed through me; I needed to get the hell out of there. Now. But a neighbor yelled at the cats through an open window and I was afraid he'd come out just when I emerged from beneath the bushes. So I stayed put.

The neighbor did come out. He threw a bucket of water on the cats and they yowled one more time and disentangled themselves. One took off running to the back of the house, the other—Jack's ginger cat—darted beneath the cypress tree, into the bushes, where she confronted me with angry meows.

Jack's front door banged, and I heard him calling in his low, whiskey voice. "Here, kitty, kitty." He clicked his tongue on the top of his mouth. "Come on now."

The cat meowed back at him.

Jack muttered something, sighed, and now I could see him heading toward the bushes where I was hiding. He parted the branches, prepared to scoop up the cat, which had by now jumped into my lap and pressed itself against my chest. Instinctively, I put my arms around her.

"Whoa!" Jack said, his face within inches of mine.

I scrambled up, nearly knocking him over. The cat leapt out of my arms and disappeared into the night. When we both caught our balance, we were face-to-face again, so close that I could smell the booze and cigarettes on his breath, the rank odor of perspiration and tobacco smoke in his clothes.

He stepped back. "Paul?" he says. "Is that you?"

"Yeah," I said. "Look, man, I'm sorry. Really. I'm sorry. I was… driving. I ended up here. And the music—" I waved toward the window. "I could hear you typing, so I just sat down under the tree so I could listen."

"You want to be a writer?" he asked, his voice weary. "Is that it?"

"No," I said. "No way."

He gave me a long look.

"Seriously. That's not why I'm here."

"Ti-Jean?" Mamère stepped out onto the little cement porch, the lapels of her pink housecoat clutched to her throat, and peered out into the yard, where we stood in the moonlight. "Ti-Jean, who is it?"

"Paul," he said. "Chuck's friend, Paul."

She spoke to him in French.

Jack turned to me. "She says, 'Come in.' She wants to feed you."

"Oh," I said. "No, it's too late. She should go back to bed. Really. I'll go now."

I took a step toward the street, but Jack put his arm around my shoulder. "Remember?" he said, not unkindly. "We don't argue with Mamére. She says she wants to feed you? You come in and be fed."

"Okay, then. Thank you," I said, and followed them inside.

She disappeared into the kitchen, and there was a clatter of pans and dishes. I sat on the couch, where Chuck and I had sat watching the Series; Jack sat in his chair. The cat reappeared, jumped up, and he cradled her in his arms like a baby, stroking her absentmindedly, looking off into space—maybe still in the world of the story he'd been typing until the catfight began, maybe listening to the music, which he hadn't turned down and which filled the tiny living room.

When it stopped, there was a flapping sound as the end of the tape disengaged from the reel, and Jack got up, the cat still in his arms, and hit a button to rewind it. In the silence left when the whirring stopped, I heard the radio playing low: a jazz station—the sad, human wail of a saxophone, and I was back, *again,* in the world of my childhood.

Would it ever stop, I wondered—this constant plummeting backward to that lost time, the happiness, the small comforts and promises I used to take for granted? It was too real. Me, drowsy in the backseat of the car, my parents' voices and the music on the radio the same thing; a late-night glimpse of Dad on the couch, his eyes closed, and Mom curled up, her head on his lap, his fingers combing her hair; Christmas morning, Dad opening the box with the record player she'd saved up to buy him.

The ding of Mamère's kitchen timer brought me back to the present, and soon afterward she emerged with two steaming plates of chicken and noodles, which she set on the table in the dining area.

"You boys eat," she said, waving us over.

A flicker of annoyance crossed Jack's face.

"You, too, Ti-Jean," she said.

Instead, he drank his glass of red wine right down, then poured himself another. Suddenly starving, I wolfed down the meal, thanking Mamère repeatedly and telling her how good it was.

She cast an accusing glance at Jack. "You eat like Paul, Ti-Jean? You feel better."

But he shook his head and pushed his plate away. The two of them watched me finish and wipe up the gravy with a piece of bread until the plate shone.

Jack poured me a second glass of wine, which I didn't really like. But I drank it, to be polite. He poured another for Mamère and for himself, as well. Then another, the two of them downing the rest of the bottle, apparently oblivious to the hour. Maybe it was the wine that made Mamère begin to cry.

Jack put his hand on hers, and spoke to her tenderly, in French.

She shook her head, dabbed at her eyes with a napkin.

I knew I should have left them alone, but I didn't know how to go. Mamère continued to cry, Jack continued to try to comfort her. I wondered if she was crying about her daughter, Nin, whose obituary in the newspaper was what had set Duke and me on the road. Her high-school picture was on the table, next to Jack's—a pretty, dark-haired girl, her face lit up with a smile. And another one, taken around the same time: Jack leaning against a porch rail, his arms folded, half of his face in shadow; Nin sitting on the rail, her hands clasped in her lap, her legs crossed at the ankles. They were so close that Jack's shoulder overlapped hers, but the effect wasn't one of closeness: the way one of his legs is bent back, resting on the bottom of the rail, made it seem as if he was in motion, walking away from her.

I felt a little light-headed from the wine, that unpleasant swirling sensation, and I wasn't sure what would happen if I tried to get up, what I might do or say. So I was glad that Jack and Mamère seemed to have forgotten that I was there, and I just sat quietly. They might have been husband and wife, I thought. Her head on his shoulder, his hand on hers, rubbing her swollen knuckles with his thumb. In time, he helped her up and into her bedroom.

"She's suffered so many losses," he said, when he came back. "No mother should ever lose a child to death. My sister, just weeks ago. My brother, when he was just nine."

"Gerard," I said. "Chuck lent me your book about him. It was really sad."

Jack lit a cigarette, takes a long drag. "He was an extraordinary child. The nuns sat with him, taking down the visions that came to him when he was dying. You don't get over such losses."

"My mom died," I said. "Last spring."

I hadn't meant to say it, and now that I had I expected the usual awkward condolence. Instead, Jack looked at me and said, "And you will never get over it. It's not meant for us to get over that kind of sadness."

His words—kind, but so matter-of-fact—ricocheted like pinballs in my head.

You'll be okay, people had said when Mom died. *Time heals all wounds. You're strong. You'll get over this. Sadness doesn't last forever.*

They hadn't been lying. They believed this and wanted me to believe it, too. They believed it would be a comfort to me. But I couldn't believe it. I didn't believe it now. I'd never get over my mom's death, not really. I'd known it from the moment Dad came into the hospital waiting room and told Bobby and me that she had a brain tumor. It was a relief to let the knowledge out of the heavy locked box inside me, let it flood through me. I felt like I used to feel, bursting to the surface in the swimming pool when I'd been testing myself to see how long I could stay underwater.

And, suddenly, I saw that *this* was what Kerouac knew. *This* was what I had come searching for, though I couldn't have known it when Duke and I set out that night in September.

It was also the wildness in *On the Road*.

Not rebellion, not good times. Not even beatitude, like some people thought—or not only that. The wildness was Jack losing his brother when he was a little boy and never getting over it. It's the noise of the world escalating in his increasingly frantic attempts to drown out the inner voice saying, *You will never stop grieving for what you've lost.*

Now he put his rough hand on mine, leaned toward me, speaking of the comfort only Our Lord could bring in the face of such sadness. His words were slurred and urgent; his voice broke.

"Your mother, she's with Him now, in heaven," he said. "Beyond pain and suffering, alive again in divine ecstasy. She waits for you, all the blessed souls in heaven wait and watch over us, angels, who know now that life on earth is no more than illusion, that the sorrows of death mean nothing, *nothing* in the face of eternal life in heaven with our Savior."

His eyes filled with tears, his hands shook as he took the bottle from its place between the cushions of his chair, uncapped it, and drank from it. He closed his eyes, murmuring what might have been a prayer, his voice growing fainter and fainter until, with a sigh, his body loosened and he slept—beneath the crucifix, the cat purring on his chest.

I re-capped the bottle that had fallen from his hand and tucked it back into place, took the ever-present cigarette from between his fingers and stubbed it out, then left quietly to begin the next leg of my journey, which Jack couldn't help me with. The part in which I'd have to learn how to live with what I knew.

TWENTY-FOUR

As I drove through silent streets, back to the main part of town, my whole life ran through my mind. Everything. I'd heard people say that happened when your life was in imminent danger. But what I felt was the sudden absence of danger, the world righting itself inside me. The sad memories were still sad; they always would be. But the happy memories weren't so freighted with loss—and, for the first time since Mom had died, I began to imagine the kind of family Dad and Bobby and I might become.

I hadn't mentioned Thanksgiving when I talked to Dad. I still wasn't ready to feel what I knew I would feel seeing him and Bobby again. But I *would* ask him to come down and visit soon. Christmas, maybe. I could see the two of them stretched out on the lounge chairs at The Palms: Dad in the awful plaid Bermuda shorts he broke out maybe twice a year, under duress; Bobby in his football jersey and ratty White Sox cap. Lo fussing over them, bringing Dad high balls, Bobby bottles of freezing cold Coke. Dean Martin, Frank Sinatra, and Sammy Davis, Jr. records dropping, one by one, on the hi-fi.

It was after midnight now. I was pretty sure Chuck would let me into the Y, but I wasn't ready to go in yet. I needed some time just to be alone. So I drove over to the parking lot across from the pier where Ginny always parked. I turned off the engine, reclined the seat as far back as it would go, lay back, and closed my eyes. My body ached with exhaustion. I could hear the ocean, and I breathed the rhythm of tide moving wave by wave toward the shore. Half-asleep, half-awake, I felt the presence of my mom in the endless motion of the water; the salty air on my face felt like her fingers brushing my hair back from my forehead like she used to do when I was little, just after she'd kissed me goodnight.

I guess I fell asleep, because the next thing I heard was Ginny's voice. "Paul? *Paul!*" She rocked my shoulder until I stirred and opened my eyes.

For a moment, I didn't know where I was. I rubbed my eyes with the heels of my hands and opened them again.

I was in the driver's seat of Ginny's car; she was in the seat beside me. It was still dark, with a sprinkling of stars in the sky.

"What time is it?" I asked.

"Two-thirty. Chuck was worried when you didn't come in, so he called me. I thought you might come here and just wait for Jimmy to come in, so I borrowed my mom's car and drove over."

"Oh, shit," I said. "Listen, I'm really—"

"I know, I know. But would you just tell me why you didn't go back to the Y? Did you call your dad? Did something happen?"

"I called him," I said. "We talked. And then, I don't know, I just really missed him. And my brother. I got this weird idea that I needed to go sit by Jack Kerouac's house for a while, like it would help me think and—"

Suddenly, I was crying. The whole story tumbled out of me: the voices, the catfight, the warmed-up chicken and noodles, Jack and his mother drunk and wrecked, him saying to me, *And you'll never get over it*—and how that was such a comfort to me, the *only* comfort anyone had given.

Ginny listened. At some point, she put her hand on mine, and, instinctively, my palm turned up, grasped it, and I held on hard.

Maybe too hard, I realized. But when I loosened my grip for fear I might be hurting her, she held on tight.

We sat like that, for a long time after I finished talking. I wasn't crying anymore, but my body was shuddering, my breathing was jagged. What I wanted to do was go back to sleep, pretend I hadn't just totally lost it in front of Ginny.

Of course, she knew what I was thinking; sometimes I thought she knew everything. "It's okay," she said. "It's good. You needed to get all that crap out.

"Breathe!" she ordered.

I breathed. I *could.* I felt space opening up inside me, my heart expanding into it.

"Good," she said again.

I looked at her. She looked at me.

She smiled and gave me that familiar little punch on my arm.

"Come on," she said. "We need to call Chuck."

And heading for the Crab Shack, still holding Ginny's hand, I felt grounded in a way I'd never felt before, not even when I was a little kid, happy, safe inside my family, no idea whatsoever about how much life could change me or who I might turn out to be. Not that I knew all that much now. But I knew that staying grounded, making a good life for myself, required the opposite of forgetting Mom's illness and her death. It wasn't about forgetting Kathy, either, or how I'd hurt her. It wasn't even about forgetting how I'd just taken off with Duke without saying goodbye.

Sadness and grief and recklessness had brought me to this moment. But so had the happy times when Mom was alive, and those nights by the river with Kathy, and Duke and I, ravenous, running for the diner that first morning on the road. The kindness of strangers along the way, and even the trouble. The tender touch of a mermaid in the quiet of her room. Everything, everyone would live inside me forever. I would carry them with me, one foot in the present world and one in the past. Breathing in the cool salty air in a place I was just starting to know, I was instantly carried back to a summer day in Indiana, playing baseball with my brother in our neighbor's backyard: the crack of the bat, the ball rising against the blue sky, and me already running, arm raised and reaching, so sure where it would land that I could already feel it slap against my glove.

ACKNOWLEDGMENTS

First and foremost, thanks to Skip Berry who kindly gave me the idea for this book after he decided he didn't want to use it himself.

Thanks to the Indiana Arts Commission for a grant that allowed me to take the road trip Duke and Paul took, and to Joan Warrick for coming along for the ride.

Thanks to the Ragdale Foundation for time to work on this book in a lovely, peaceful place.

Thanks to Dan Wakefield for his encouragement.

Thanks to Victoria Barrett and Andrew Scott, publisher and editor extraordinaire. I can't imagine two better stewards for a book.

Thanks to my family: Steve, Kate, Jenny, Heidi, Jake, Jim, and Olivier.

And to my sisters' families: Diny, Hud, Dan, Sam, David, Chris, Ben, Katie, Christine, Kylie, and the first of the new batch of babies, Jack.

As Sam once said in the worst of times, "We are a kickass family."

In memory of Jackie Weitz (1952–2003).
We miss you so much.

ABOUT THE AUTHOR

 **BARBARA SHOUP** is the author of seven previous novels. Her short fiction, poetry, essays, and interviews have appeared in numerous outlets, including *The Writer* and the *New York Times*. *Wish You Were Here* and *Stranded in Harmony* were selected as American Library Association Best Books for Young Adults. *Vermeer's Daughter* was a *School Library Journal* Best Adult Book for Young Adults. Shoup was the 2006 recipient of the PEN/Phyllis Naylor Working Writer Fellowship, and her books have received numerous awards. She is the Executive Director of the Indiana Writers Center and lives in Indianapolis.

Author photograph by Freddi Stevens-Jacobi